WITSEC

USMS MARSHAL THRILLER SERIES

JODI BURNETT

SDG PUBLISHING

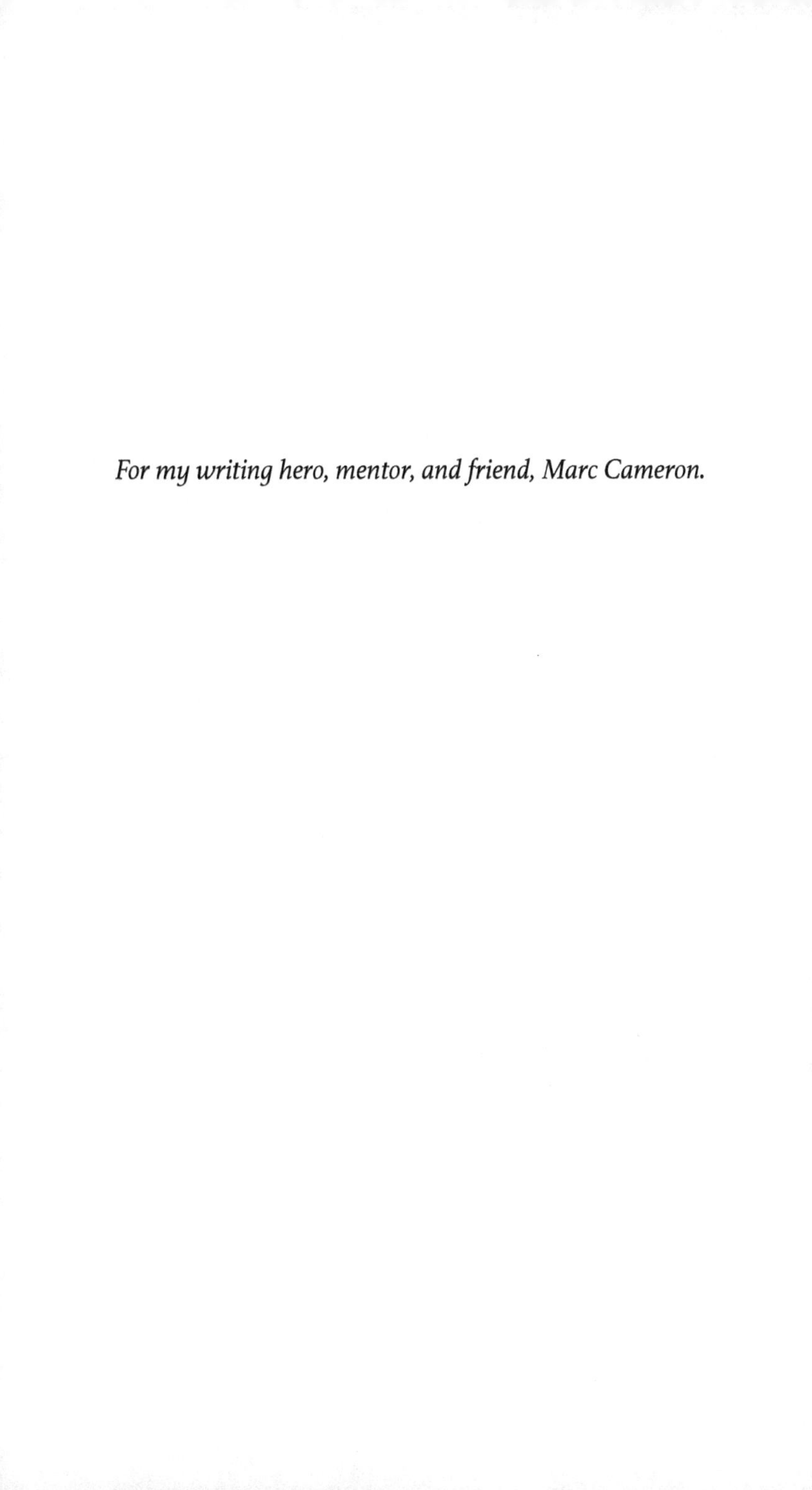

For my writing hero, mentor, and friend, Marc Cameron.

WITSEC

PROLOGUE

Melissa Bennington popped a sugary sweet bubble in her chewing gum as she twisted a length of her best friend Karis's hair into a French braid. "You do too, like him," Melissa teased. "You're such a liar."

Karis pulled away, spinning toward Melissa, the plait unwinding from her dark brown tresses. "I do not! God! I can't believe you, Mel."

"Yes, you do!" Allegra, another one of the five fifteen-year-old girls at the slumber party, shouted. With a waft of her Victoria Secret's Bombshell scent, she swatted Karis with a cushion and then reached for her phone. "Look how often you post on Cooper's page!"

"Shut up, you guys." Karis shoved Allegra back with the pillow, knocking her off the family room couch. Laughing at the slender blonde with her feet in the air; Karis held a hand out to help her up. "You can't tell anyone, you guys. I mean it!"

Esme, whose party it was, tossed a handful of

popcorn at Karis. "You're such a dumbass, Kar! Everyone *already* knows. Especially Cooper!"

Karis's cheeks flamed with embarrassment, and Melissa took pity on her. "It's true, Kar-bear, but so what? He likes you, too. It's so obvi!"

Karis buried her face in her hands. "He does not... does he?" She peeked out. "Why do you say that? Did he say something?"

Esme's mom entered the family room which her decorator had designed in a casual, but elegant look, with creams and blues that suited the large Nantucket-style colonial home located in the affluent Ridgefield, Connecticut neighborhood. She called out, "Hey girls, we're going to go get the pizza and some snacks. Behave while we're gone, okay?"

"And don't break anything," Esme's dad chuckled as he guided his wife toward the door.

"Mom! Don't forget the Mountain Dew," Esme hollered after her parents half a second before another pillow bashed into her head.

Poppy, the tallest of the girls, and captain of the cheer squad, giggled when the blow knocked Karis off balance, causing her to trip over a tufted leather ottoman and fall on her butt. "Hey, you guys! Let's stalk Cooper on Insta."

Melissa carefully stuffed any signs of the jealousy swelling hot and prickly in her chest. Even though she was currently dating Fletcher Gibbons, she'd had a secret crush on Cooper Williams since third grade. But he barely noticed her. Karis was the one he wanted to ask out. Cooper was a junior and had recently gotten his driver's license. Melissa used to fantasize all the time about driving around with him in his new red Toyota Tacoma.

That was until Fletcher asked her out. The first time Fletch kissed her she couldn't catch her breath. She finally knew what true love was. She still shivered at the memory. There would never be anyone else for her. Melissa leaned over the back of the couch to look at Poppy's phone screen. Melissa's bladder complained it was full, but she ignored the warning, not wanting to miss anything.

Poppy copied Cooper's profile picture and then added silly filters to his face, threatening to post the one with floppy dog ears and a black nose she had imposed over his features. Laughing, Melissa crossed her legs and bounced on the couch cushion, no longer able to put off her body's insistent urging. "I'll be right back," she announced to the girls, but no one noticed as she skipped off to the powder room in the hallway.

She closed the door behind her and studied her reflection in the mirror. The zit in the crease of her nose was redder than the last time she checked, but she didn't have her cover-up with her. Sighing, she did her business. While she re-tied the cord on her pink flannel pajama bottoms, a bang echoed from somewhere in the house that was so loud it shook the walls. Her friends screamed, and two comically Slavic accented men's voices yelled over their shrieks.

"Everybody, shut up and keep your hands where we can see them! Drop the damn phone!" One of the girls in the other room started crying. "Where is your father?"

Melissa's heart rate catapulted as she listened to the

commotion from behind the bathroom door. Sobbing, Esme answered. "He... they... who are you?"

The deeper of the men's voices growled, "Is he home or not?"

"No," Esme whimpered.

Melissa wondered if this was a prank dreamed up by Cooper and his friends. The guys knew they were having a sleepover. At least they should know. She and the other girls had been dropping tons of hints all week long in the hope the boys might crash their party. Silently, Melissa cracked opened the bathroom door and peeked out. She turned on her phone's video camera to film the dramatic effects of their joke.

Two male forms, dressed in black and wearing matching ski masks, stood at the entrance to the room. They held realistic-looking toy guns pointed at the gaggle of pajama-clad girls. Melissa couldn't tell if her friends were truly scared or just playing along for fun.

Allegra laughed. "We know it's you, Coop. You can't fool us!" She sprang toward the shorter man on the right and snatched off his knit head covering. A look of surprised horror washed over her face as everyone real-ized the man holding them at gunpoint was not Cooper, or any of the other boys they went to school with. Allegra screamed, and the guy aimed his pistol at her and fired. The bullet made a zipping sound before a red explosion splashed against the wall behind her. Allegra crumpled to the white carpet beneath her. The gun was clearly not a toy.

Melissa slapped a hand over her mouth so she wouldn't scream as her friends in the other room shrieked in terror. The second man, with his mask still in place, yelled, "What the hell, Pavlo? You idiot! Now they can identify you."

The bare-faced man yanked at his partner's face-covering, tearing it from his head. "Yeah, well, now they can recognize you, too."

"You are so stupid, Pavlo! We can't leave witnesses who can point us out in a line-up and lead the cops back to Volodymyr. He will kill us without a second thought."

Poppy lunged at the man called Pavlo, but his partner caught her by her hair and flung her backward across the room. She crashed against the foot of an armchair, and he shot her before she could scream.

He then raised his weapon and fired two more spitting shots. Silence filled the house but rang in Melissa's ears. Her body trembled so violently it was difficult to get her fingers to work as she texted the video to her mom's phone. Tears poured down her cheeks, but she dared not make a sound. Gently, she pulled the door closed and slowly released the handle before locking it.

In alarm, one of the killers growled, "What was that? Did you hear it?"

"What?'

"A click. Something. It came from the hallway."

Melissa's muscles tensed with fear as she looked frantically around the room for anything she could use for self-defense. Neither the toilet brush nor the toilet-paper stand would help her. Her only chance was to climb out the window. She pushed at the sash, but it was stuck to the paint on the sill. She grabbed the toilet brush and leveraged its handle between the pane and the latch to pry the glass open.

The knob rattled behind her. The killers were on the other side of the bathroom door! Her flimsy pry bar slipped, crushing her fingers against the frame. She shook out her hand and tried again. The paint sealing the opening stretched before it gave, and finally the window came loose. Melissa shoved open the sash and tore the screen away. She pressed her hands against the sill, lifting her body up. She leaned out the window, but in the darkness, she couldn't see how far it was to the ground below. Holding the two side buttons on both sides of her phone down, she called 911 seconds before she pushed herself farther out the small opening. One of the burglars kicked in the entrance. The frame splintered, and the heavy wooden door crashed into the wall behind it before slamming shut again on the rebound. The man in the hallway cussed and growled in frustration.

Melissa had no time. She dove, tumbling head-first from the window, landing in a row of shrubs fifteen feet below. Her phone flew from her hand when she hit, leaving her without light. Branches cut and scratched her arms, stinging her in the frosty night air. Barefoot, she sprinted across the frozen lawn to the back of the house, disappearing into the surrounding woods.

Heavy footsteps chased her into the darkness. Melissa couldn't outrun the men, so she dove into a thicket of shrubs and crawled beneath the undergrowth. Black boots came to a halt inches from her face, and she held her breath.

One of her pursuers called out, "Andriy! There's a car pulling into the drive."

"Let's go finish this."

The boots pivoted and pounded away on the cold ground. Her pursuer sprinted back toward the house. Melissa gasped for the air her lungs demanded. Two more shots echoed in the night. Although tears poured from her eyes, terror paralyzed her limbs. Finally, sirens sounded in the distance, shaking her from her self-imposed coma, and she climbed to her feet and ran.

Volodymyr Kovalenko drew on his traditional thin silver Ukrainian pipe, letting the flavor of tobacco roll across his tongue as he gazed out at the cold gray New England sky and listened to the men in his home office standing before his desk, wringing their hands and whining. He smoothed and twisted the end of his salt and pepper mustache up as he waited for them to finish their shameful version of what had happened at the Davis house in Connecticut. Anger flickered in his belly like the fire blazing on the hearth as the two buffoons blamed everyone and everything but themselves for their enormous blunder.

He pulled the antique pipe—a gift from his adoptive father and mentor, Boris Orlov, leader of the Mashkov Syndicate in Brighton Beach—from between his lips and let the smoke from his lungs rise in front of his face. "So, you are telling me we have six dead people and an eyewitness to your idiocy on our hands?"

The men glanced between each other and then dropped their gaze to the intricate Turkish carpet under their feet. Finally, Pavlo answered, "Yes, sir."

"Well, now you must fix it." Volodymyr gripped the arm of his leather chair and leaned forward. "Find the girl."

Andriy, the stronger of the two, swallowed. "We don't know where she went, Boss. And we had to get out of there before the cops showed up. At least we capped Davis and his wife. Your message to those who owe you money was loud and clear."

Pavlo nodded his agreement like a bobble-head doll. "Yeah, Boss. Loud and clear. Nobody's gonna try to cheat you out of what they owe, ever again."

Kovalenko kept his tone low and menacing. "If the police find the girl before you do, we will all spend the rest of our lives in prison. Find her, damn you!"

Andriy opened his mouth to utter what Volodymyr assumed was another lame excuse, but his Kapitan, Mishka Fomichev, stepped forward, and staring at his phone, he pushed the underling aside. "The teenage girls posted many photographs of their party on social media before you imbeciles got there." He tapped his screen. "After identifying the girls who were killed, I discovered the lone survivor. The girl we're searching for is tagged in the party posts. Her name is Melissa Bennington." He showed the image to Kovalenko. "She's the pretty one with long brown hair."

Volodymyr pressed a thin smile onto his lips. "Good. Now, find her, and dispose of her."

1

———

US Deputy Marshal Dirk Sterling waited in his black Jeep Rubicon for his partner, Hank Flannigan, as the vehicle's engine warmed in the eighteen-degree morning. When neither of them had plans after work, they'd taken to carpooling ever since Hank had sought refuge at Dirk's house from his crumbling marriage with Amy. Dirk tapped his fingers on the steering wheel, impatient to get on the road.

Finally, Hank came out of the house. Steam rose both from his insulated mug and his recently coiffed hair. Dirk liked to tease the kid about the trendy blond swirl he often sported above his forehead. Hank got into the Jeep, filling the car with the rich scent of coffee, and Dirk grumbled, "You take longer to get ready than any woman I've ever known. Did you get your Dairy Queen hair-do just right?"

Hank chuckled. "You're just jealous. It takes effort to be as good-looking as me and you're just not willing to put in the work."

"Yeah. That's it." Dirk smirked and shook his head.

Hank set his coffee in the cup holder and snapped on his belt. "It surprised me when you said you didn't have plans tonight. Aren't you and the chief getting together?"

"We're slowing things down a little." Dirk's chest tightened. He did not want to hash through his and Emory's relationship with Hank. It was a sore subject, and frankly, one he'd rather not think about at all.

"Oh, yeah? Why's that?"

Dirk sighed as he merged onto I-90 toward downtown Billings. "We're not sure we want the same things. No big deal."

Hank's brows drew together. "Right. Like I believe that. Are we still on for Thanksgiving dinner at her place?"

"Yeah, only it's going to be at my house instead, since I have more room. If your wife comes, we'll have ten people."

Hank pressed his head back on the car seat and closed his eyes. "She still hasn't decided if she's coming or not. Our marriage counselor thinks it would be a good idea, but Amy thinks everyone who will be there is on my side."

Dirk wanted to keep the conversation positive. "How's she feeling? She's what, three months along now?"

"Four. Her doctor says she should feel better in the mornings during the middle trimester."

Dirk turned and exited the highway. "When did you say the baby's due date is?"

A wide grin slid across Hank's face. "End of April, around the twenty-ninth."

Dirk laughed. He was happy for the kid, but he wished things were smoother between him and his wife. "Are you and Amy going to hang in there until after the baby is born?"

"That's what our counselor recommends. But things aren't getting any better between us. I think the separation is only solidifying the idea that we're happier apart. She has her mom and I... well, I'm happier not getting yelled at all the time."

Dirk nodded but kept his thoughts to himself as he pulled into the parking lot behind the US Marshals building. He glanced up and saw Emory watching them from her office window above. There was no question that he loved her, and he missed seeing her every night. His heart ached at the thought. The uncertainty lay in whether they could make a future together when she wanted kids, and he absolutely did not.

Dirk tossed his black leather jacket on the back of his desk chair and turned to greet his boss and lover, Emory Grey. She had pulled her long blonde hair into a no-nonsense bun at her nape. His gaze panned down over her figure swathed in a plum-colored suit whose skirt skimmed her knees. As his eyes rose again to her face, a smile followed. "Good morning, Chief."

"Good morning, Dirk... Henry." She was the only one on the team who used Hank's formal name. "The morning meeting will be at ten o'clock rather than nine, today. I have a Zoom meeting to attend." Her tone was chilly, but her gaze lingered on Dirk for a few seconds before she returned to her office.

He longed to follow her and close the door behind

him, but Dirk reminded himself that he was the one who wanted to cool things off for a while. Instead, he went to the break room. Passing Teresa Mendez at her desk, he asked, "Hey, T, want a cup of coffee?"

"Sure. Thanks." Teresa, though as much of a deputy marshal as the rest of them, worked as the office admin. She made the choice to stay in the office, so that as a single mom, she would have a safer job with a more regular schedule. That way she could better care for her eight-year-old son, Tomas. "I sent you guys an email with the latest list of dirt-bags to hunt down."

"Music to my ears." Dirk found the coffee pot half-full, poured two cups, and made another pot. He added sugar and cream to one mug and took it to Teresa.

She took a sip. "Ah... just how I like it."

Hank leaned back in his chair as he studied his computer monitor. "Teresa, can you filter this list by last known location or even by the site of the crimes? This list is all over the map."

"Yeah, I can. Hold on." She clicked away on her keyboard. "Dirk likes to see the worst criminals first, so that's what I sent you." She gave her keys one last hard tap. "There you go."

Dirk pressed his mouse. "Got it. Hank, pick your top three from the list T just emailed. I'll choose mine from the other. Then we can get to work on hunting these scum balls down." They spent the next hour researching their new targets.

Emory came out of her office carrying a large bakery box. "Time for our meeting. I brought us some chocolate croissants."

Dirk pushed away from his desk. "That's one way to bribe us to attend the meeting." Following Emory, he reached around her to snatch a pastry from the box. "I didn't have breakfast."

Emory swatted at his hand. "At least wait till I set the box down," she laughed and called over her shoulder, "Can someone bring the coffee?"

Once everyone had settled with their iPads, croissants, and coffees, Emory started the meeting. Dirk was prepared to give a brief on two criminals he thought they could track down, but the chief took the conversation in another direction. He licked a few buttery flakes from his fingertips and listened.

"Before I give my briefing and hear what you have on your plates, we've had a sudden change in plans. One of the JPAT 727s is landing at Logan International at eleven-thirty this morning. They are escorting a family who has been entered into the Witness Security Program. Dirk, you and Henry need to meet the plane and drive the family to their new home here in Billings."

Hank sprang forward, sloshing coffee onto his jeans. "Crap!" He brushed at the spill with a napkin. "Sorry. Doesn't WITSEC handle their own witness relocation?"

Emory lifted several napkins from a stack next to the bakery box and handed them to Hank. "They usually get witnesses settled in, but it's common for local marshal's offices to monitor them after that. In this case, JPAT needs their plane elsewhere and asked if we'd do them the favor."

Dirk bit into his rich, flakey pastry and closed his eyes briefly as he savored the butter and chocolate flavors blending in his mouth. He swallowed and wiped some left-over crumbs from his lips. "Hey, Hank. You were a pilot in the Army. Why didn't you apply to the Justice Prisoner and Alien Transportation System? You could have been a pilot *and* a deputy."

"I didn't want to just fly prisoners around. I wanted to hunt them down."

Dirk chuckled. "That's my boy. I feel the same way." He turned a hard gaze toward Emory. "We shouldn't be babysitting a WITSEC family when we could be out tracking dangerous criminals. This seems like the perfect job for Teresa." He glanced at the admin. "No offense, T."

"None taken." Teresa licked chocolate from her fingers. "But no can do today. Tomas has an awards ceremony this afternoon that I am not missing."

"Dirk, this is the job. It's not all shoot 'em up cowboy stuff. Today, you and Hank are going to welcome this family to Billings." Emory turned on the smart board and images of the family covered the space. "Now, the teenage daughter is an eyewitness to multiple murders. She watched as two members, whom the FBI has confirmed are from a Ukrainian crime family in New Jersey, shot and killed four of her friends at a slumber party. She had left the room to go to the bathroom when two men broke into the house and killed the others. Fortunately, she escaped with her life through the bathroom window. But as she ran away, she heard two more gunshots. Investigators report those shots killed the parents who had returned home with pizza for the sleepover. Investigating agents from the FBI believe the killers were sent to murder the father because he owed the Ukrainians hundreds of thousands of dollars, but when they got there, they found themselves in the middle of a slumber party and panicked. The surviving witness has identified the killers in a lineup and will testify against them in court when the time comes. Until then, we are going to help her, and her family adjust to their new lives here in Billings."

Dirk tapped his electronic pen against the top of his tablet. "Whatever you say, boss. What are the family's new names?"

"They are now the Miller family. They lived in Ridgefield, Connecticut." A photo of a man in a well-tailored business suit lit the screen. "The father was a heavy-hitting investment broker in New York City. He's now James Miller, a tax accountant in Billings."

"Ouch." Hank reached for a second pastry. "That has to hurt."

Emory continued. "This is Ann Miller." An image of a beautiful brunette standing behind the steering wheel on a yacht, laughing into the wind, took the place of her husband. "Early forties. Technically, a stay-at-home mom, but she does... did... a lot of charitable work."

Emory clicked to the next slide. A fifteen-year-old version of the mother appeared. "This is Kendall. She's the witness. Poor girl is pretty messed up. We will set her up with a USMS-approved therapist." One more click, and two images filled the board. "These are Kendall's brothers. The older boy is thirteen. His name is Jack. Jack was a big name in competitive baseball in Connecticut, but unfortunately, being in WITSEC prevents him from pursuing the sport here. Which, of course, has already become an issue within the family. And the younger boy is Joe. He's eight, and the WITSEC liaison reports that Joe thinks this is all a grand adventure. He'll be the hardest to handle as far as keeping their cover a secret." Emory set the remote down. "Any questions?"

"Yeah, what all do Dirk and I have to do after we meet them at the airport?"

"You'll drive them to their new home and help them get settled. One of you will need to make a grocery run while the other can stay at the home with the Millers to answer questions and assist in any way."

Dirk chuffed. "It's basic baby-sitting, kid. Just what you always wanted to do when you grew up."

Irritation sparked in Emory's emerald-green eyes, and she pursed her lips at him. "Don't worry, Dirk. Your beloved, Most Wanted list will be here waiting on your desk for you when you return. All I'm asking is one day."

"I guess you could convince me with another croissant."

Emory reached in the box for a pastry and practically threw it at him. Laughing, he caught it one-handed. "Come on, Hank. We better get out of here before the chief starts a food fight."

2

Teresa printed out the alternative names and new address for the Bennington family, now known as the Millers. She read the pages as they came out of the printer. A swish of a pen transformed Marc Bennington, the investment broker, into James the tax accountant, Tiffany the socialite became Ann, a stay-at-home mom looking for work. Melissa, a cheerleader and one of the most popular girls at her high school in Connecticut, now became Kendall the new girl in town who missed her friends desperately, who was unfortunately dealing with major survivor's guilt along with the crushing sense that she'd ruined her family's lives. None of her feelings she could share outside of her own family and her assigned USMS therapist.

The family's assumed identity forced Easton, a young man with a true future in baseball, to become Jack, a talented athlete who could not go anywhere near a ball diamond. And then there was Asher, who was now Joey. At least he was content with the latest turn in his life. At eight, he was young enough that the changes he faced likely seemed like a game.

Teresa handed the sheet of information to Dirk as he and Hank left the office. "Good luck. You have two teenagers on this list who will probably prove to be a handful."

"Yeah, thanks." Dirk folded the paper and slid it into an inside pocket of his leather jacket and joined Hank at the elevator.

Teresa returned to the conference room to help Emory tidy up after their meeting. "I've assisted with WITSEC before, but never with an entire family. It's always been a single adult, or maybe a couple." She took the last remaining bite of her croissant and licked the creamy chocolate frosting from her fingertips.

Emory tossed the used napkins in the trash. "I'm sure it'll be rough for them. Although at least they have each other to lean on." She closed the box lid on the left-over pastries. "You know, Teresa, their youngest son is regis-tered to attend the same elementary school that Tomas goes to."

"Really? Is their house in my neighborhood?" Teresa picked up the four coffee mugs and headed to the break room to set them in the sink.

Emory followed her, placing the croissants on the counter for later. "No, they'll live in a house on the other side of the school from your place. But Tomas will probably cross paths with Joey. They're the same age."

"Is he going to be in Tomas's class?" Teresa didn't know how she felt about that. Though Joey wasn't the specific target of the New Jersey crime family, he still represented the possibility of danger.

"I don't have any information about that. Eight-year-olds are in third grade, right? How many third-grade classrooms are there in Tomas's school?"

"Two, I think." Teresa poured herself the remainder of the coffee and warmed her mug in the microwave.

"This could be a good thing. You're probably at the school enough that you could keep an eye out for Joey."

Teresa's gut twisted. She didn't like the idea of her work involving Tomas. If the boys became friends, she'd have to lie to her own son about what she knew, and that didn't sit well. "Isn't the family hiding from a Ukrainian mob family? Honestly, Chief, I don't want that kind of threat anywhere near Tomas's life."

"I understand your hesitation, but Joey is not the one the mob is after. They probably don't even know he exists. I just like the idea of several pairs of eyes on the family, making sure they are settling in. A little guy like Joey could get lost in the shuffle."

Her boss's reasoning made sense, but Teresa couldn't shake her discomfort. Not to mention her irritation with being asked to blur the lines between her home life and work. "I'll think about it."

"Fair enough." Emory smiled at her and squeezed her shoulder. "Listen, I have a lunch meeting today, so you'll be manning the office. Text me if Dirk or Henry call in, especially if they need anything. I'm hoping the Millers will settle in easily."

"No problem." Teresa went to her desk and waited for Emory to leave. She planned to spend the afternoon prioritizing the most-wanted list the way she knew Dirk liked it. Hank could organize his copy from there. But first, she wanted to talk to Dirk and get his advice on the awkward situation the chief had put her in.

As soon as Teresa heard the elevator doors close behind her boss, she dialed Dirk.

"What's up, T?"

"Hey, have you met the family yet?"

"Nope, we're still about ten minutes from the airport."

"So... the chief told me the youngest boy, Joey, will attend Tomas's elementary school."

"Huh."

"Yeah. I already don't like that, but then she asked if I'd keep an eye on the kid."

"She probably means from afar. Not that you have to spy on him or something."

"I guess. But Joey is the same age as Tomas. He could wind up in his class. What if they become friends? Then I'd feel like I was lying to Tomas. Not to mention the potential danger Joey brings with him. I just don't like it. What do you think?"

"I hear you, T, but the kid isn't the one at risk. It's his big sister we need to worry about. Even if Tomas and Joey became friends, you wouldn't be lying if you simply said nothing. Besides, there are a lot of what-ifs and maybes taking place in your imagined scenario. They may not even like each other. Who knows?"

"I suppose you're right. I'm making a bigger deal out of this than I need to. But what bothers me the most is that the chief asked me to blur the lines between work and home. I try to keep Tomas insulated from what I do."

"You're just being a mama bear. You're a great mom, T. But in this case, I think you're overthinking it."

"Maybe... The jury is out."

"If you decide you don't want to check in on Joey, I'm sure Emory will understand. If the kid went to a different school, we wouldn't have an inside view, and it would be fine. The decision is yours, but like I said, don't waste any brain cells worrying about it."

"Yeah. Thanks, Dirk."

"No problem. I gotta go, though. We're pulling up to the hangar now." Dirk ended the call.

Teresa agreed. She was probably making a big deal out of nothing. If only she could get the spiders crawling around in her gut to agree.

3

———

Dirk pulled to a stop outside the hangar used by the USMS JPAT 727 at Billings-Logan International Airport when they were in town. The family of five entering witness protection stood uncertainly at the side of the plane, waiting for their luggage and listening to the deputy marshal who accompanied them. Dirk and Hank stepped out of the Rubicon and approached the group.

"You must be the Millers." Dirk shook the husband's hand. The man's barely concealed anger was written all over his body. His wife also wore a scowl and kept her arms crossed firmly over her chest.

"Welcome to Billings." Dirk introduced himself and Hank. "We're your local deputy marshal liaison here to drive you to your new house and help you get settled in."

He left Hank to get acquainted with the family while he signed the transfer paperwork and talked with the family's USMS escort. "Any problems I should know about?"

"Heads up. No one in this crew is thrilled about having to take on a new identity. The parents argued the entire way here. The girl is sullen and hasn't said a single word, and the older boy might be problematic. He's angry about the change and has no problem sharing his feelings about it. Fortunately, the little kid seems fine—but who knows?"

Dirk appraised the family from a distance as his partner attempted to engage them. "Sounds about right. Did you arrange for transportation? I don't have enough room in my car for all of them."

"Yeah, a minivan should be here somewhere. They have a ton of luggage, though, so two vehicles will be a good thing." He took the clipboard with the official paperwork from Dirk. "Sorry to drop them on you and push you out, but we're collecting a fugitive transfer here in an hour and you need to be gone before then."

"No problem. We'll get these folks on their way." Dirk walked back to Hank and the family. "Let's pack as many bags as we can into my Jeep." As he said this, the expected minivan pulled into the hangar. "Here's your vehicle, Hank. You drive the van with the Millers to their new house, and I'll follow you."

The mother pressed her older son's shoulder, directing him toward their car, but he jerked away from her and stepped closer to Dirk. "Can I ride with you? I've had about all the family togetherness I can stand for one day."

Dirk shifted a questioning gaze at the mom. She nodded, so Dirk opened the passenger door. "Sure, kid. Hop in and buckle up."

Mr. Miller kept his head down as he scrolled on his phone, ignoring his family. His wife, clearly a control freak, straightened her daughter's collar before prodding her and the youngest son toward their vehicle. "Come on, Marc. It's time to go. Can't you pry your eyes from your screen for even *one* minute? Besides," curling her lip at her husband, she pushed her shoulders back and glanced at Dirk, "I'm pretty sure you're not supposed to be connected to anything from our past."

Miller cocked his jaw sideways as he slid his phone into his pocket. "You mean like the use of our old names? Aren't you supposed to be calling me *James?*"

She rolled her eyes. "Whatever. Just get in the car." She returned her gaze to Dirk. "This is going to take a while to get used to."

Dirk nodded, acknowledging the truth of her statement, and turned to help Hank load the remaining Louis Vuitton suitcases. "I texted you the address in case we get separated. I'll see you at the new house. Good luck!"

The Millers' home was roughly fifteen minutes away from the airport. On the short drive, Dirk asked Jack how all the changes were going for him.

The kid slammed his head back against the seat. "Well, I was on track to get a baseball scholarship, and now I'm not even allowed to pick up a bat. How do you think it's going? It's like we're all being punished because of what Melissa saw. It really sucks."

"I know it's hard, man." The weight of the kid's predicament pressed down on Dirk's shoulders. "But the other option is the mob finds your sister, *Kendall*, and kills her along with the rest of you—just to send a message.

It's not fair, that's true, but not much in life is. You're an athlete, no matter what. So, why not go out for another sport? Do you play football?"

Jack shook his head no, and clamping his jaw shut, he closed his eyes.

Dirk pulled to the curb in front of the Millers' new rental. Hank parked behind him, and everyone piled out of the cars. Dirk was stunned to find that by the end of the short drive, both Miller women were in tears, and Mr. Miller wore a vicious scowl. The little kid, Joey, was the only one who regarded the house with interest.

Dirk rattled the keys. "Ready to take a look inside? We can get the luggage later." He wanted to get the family off the street and away from any potential prying neighborhood eyes. They didn't need the complication of having to explain why everyone was upset the first day in their new home. He led the way up the walk and opened the front door. Joey was first to enter the house, followed by Jack's attitude and Kendall's despondency.

Kendall paused as she passed Dirk. Swiping a long silky strand of hair behind her ear, she filled his nose with her overly sweet perfume. She looked up at him. "Your partner says I can't even *look* at my old social media accounts. I don't see why. If I never click or comment, no one will know I'm there. Besides, nobody knows me by Kendall Miller, anyway."

"Unfortunately, Hank's right. I know it's tempting to see what's going on back home, and we can be sure that the men who are trying to find you hope you'll do just that. It's too risky. After what you've been through, you know what these men are capable of. For your own, and your family's sake, stay off those sites."

Kendall entered the house, whining on the way, "I miss Fletcher. And I can't believe you won't even let me see pictures of my best friends' funerals. This is so unfair!"

Ann blotted her own tears with a tissue. "We all have to make sacrifices, Mel... *Kendall*." She sighed as she studied the front of the three-bedroom ranch which was to become their home. "This house is... well, it's so small. I thought we would live in something closer to the same style to which we're accustomed."

James nudged his wife forward a little more forcefully than necessary, in Dirk's opinion. "How did you come to that conclusion, *Ann*? On Monday I have to look for a new job as a tax accountant, for god's sake, and you are going to need to find a job too, just so we can eat. No more fancy charity dinners for you, I'm afraid. Get used to it."

More tears flowed at James's bitter comments. The Miller family faced massive changes, and Dirk wondered if they'd make it. It wouldn't be the first time a family in witness protection fell apart. He and Hank followed them inside.

Dirk set down the suitcases he carried in with him. "Once you are a little settled, we're happy to drive you around Billings so you can get oriented. We'll take you to the grocery store to stock your refrigerator with some necessities."

Kendall burst into tears and ran down the hall before she realized she didn't know which room would be hers.

She looked back with teary uncertainty. "This is real. We're never going home again! We don't belong anywhere anymore!"

Flexing his jaw, James shook his head. "She's been an emotional mess since this whole thing happened."

"I bet. She's hurting." Dirk pulled his wallet from a pocket in his jacket and flipped through some business cards until he found the one he sought, and handed it to Ann. "This is the number of a US Marshal approved therapist in Billings. Kendall has gone through significant trauma, and it might help if she has someone she can talk to and be completely open and honest with. It's going to be difficult for her to deal with her pain while trying to forget her past. In fact, it'll be hard for all of you. Doctor Longsworth is an excellent resource for the whole family."

Ann accepted the card. "Thank you. And thanks for the offer of running us to the store. I know we need things, but I'm not sure my children are ready to start exploring."

Hank stepped forward. "I can stay here with the kids, if you want, while Dirk takes you around." He glanced out the picture window. "I noticed someone left a ball on the court in the park across the street. What do you say, Jack? Want to shoot some hoops while Joey plays on the playground?"

Dirk nodded at his partner. The kid was going to be a great dad. "Good idea, Hank. And Kendall, you can come with us or stay here."

Kendall sighed. "I guess I'll go with you. Can we drive by my new high school?"

4

———

The cool autumn air chilled Hank's cheeks as he crossed the street with the Miller boys. Joey ran ahead to the playground, and Jack picked up the abandoned basketball and thrust it on a hard pass to Hank, who dribbled the ball and then laid up for a basket. When Jack got the ball back, Hank noticed the boy had skills, and his movements were strong and smooth.

"I can see you're quite the athlete," Hank said, as he raised his hands high to block Jack's shot.

"*Was*, you mean."

"No, not *was*. There is no denying your natural ability. I know you played baseball before, but it's obvious you will do well in any sport you want to try. It comes naturally to you, doesn't it?"

Hank lunged to grab the basketball, but Jack was faster. He spun to the side and darted toward the hoop, making a shot that hit the backboard and dropped in.

Jack ran the ball down the court and passed it to Hank. "Maybe, but I excel at baseball. I love the game, and I might have had a real future in the sport. Now, I'm not even allowed to go out for the team." Jack stopped playing and stood with his hands on his hips in the center of the asphalt court.

"I'm sorry, Jack. That has to really suck. But the option is deadly. If the men Kendall is going to testify against hunt for your family through your talent on the field, it could lead them here to you, and... Well, we already know what they'd do."

"I know. But it's still not fair." Jack snatched the ball from Hank's hands and took a three-point shot. *Swish.* Nothing but net.

"Nice!" An odd sense of pride flowed through Hank's chest at the boy's natural abilities, which was weird since he had only just met the Millers. He wondered what it might have been like to have had little brothers or, better yet, what it would be like to have a son. His and Amy's baby was due in April, but they didn't know the gender yet. He understood it was politically correct to say it didn't matter—and it didn't, not really. But deep inside, he admitted to himself he wanted a boy. "Do you play football, too?"

"Sorta. But it's too late to go out for this year's team. They started workouts clear last summer."

"Think you'll try out for basketball?" Hank waved to Joey on the swings. He'd already made a friend at the park. Joey would have the easiest time out of the whole family adapting to his new life.

Jack shrugged and picked up the basketball. "I don't know. Where is the high school from here?"

Hank pointed north. "It's about a half a mile up the street and over a couple of blocks. We can go check it out, if you want."

"What I want is to go back home. This neighborhood sucks." Jack spiked the ball and let it bounce away. "I don't want to be the new kid. I don't want to live here."

"I know, buddy. None of this is what you would choose. I get that. But you do have a choice about how you decide to handle it. You can rail against it and be miserable, or you could look for some good things and make the best out of it. You never know, you may meet some great friends and love it here after a while."

Jack stared at Hank for a long minute. "Will I ever get to play baseball again? Like in college?"

"I can't answer that, Jack. Maybe. But definitely not as Easton Bennington. You'd be an easy target, and crime families tend to have long memories. For now, you should pick another sport to focus on."

Joey ran up the hill to the court carrying the basketball. "Here's your ball. It rolled all the way down to the slide! Can I play with you guys?"

The little boy's dark eyes glittered with hope and Hank couldn't resist his wide grin, but Jack had no such trouble. "No way, squirt. Go back to the playground."

"Come on, East—" Joey snapped his gaze to Hank. "I mean Jack. Please, can I play? Please?"

"Sure, you can." Hank ruffled Joey's light-brown hair. "Jack, I bet you could give your brother some great pointers. Let's play HORSE." Hank explained the game to Joey while Jack ignored them and practiced his free-throws.

"I get to go first." Jack made a shot from the top of the key. He ran down the ball and bounce-passed it to his little brother.

Joey used all his might to throw the ball the long distance, but it dropped short and sprang off the asphalt. His look of disappointment speared Hank's heart, so he ran to the boy and grabbed him under his arms. Lifting him, Hank ran to the ball holding Joey so he could grab it and then dashed over to the net. He held the boy up high over his head. Joey shot the ball and made the basket.

"Way to go, Joey!" Hank laughed, and Joey cheered.

Jack rolled his eyes with a disgusted attitude perfected by teenagers worldwide. "That's cheating."

"Nah, it's just having fun. You should try it." Hank took the ball to the starting point and fired it toward the basket. He missed. "Okay, Jack and Joey, you both have an H."

Joey retrieved the ball. "Your turn, Jack!"

Dirk's jeep rolled to a stop in front of the Millers' new home. Hank held up his hands for the ball. "Your folks just got back. Let's go help carry the groceries in."

"Yeah!" Joey cheered. "I bet Mom bought us some snacks!" He took off toward the house, and Jack and Hank followed.

The Millers carried their shopping bags inside while Dirk and Hank hung back. "How'd it go with the boys?"

Hank grinned. "It was fun, for the most part. But Jack is an angry kid. He had to give up some big dreams when they left their life in Connecticut. It might help for him to see the therapist, too."

Dirk rubbed the back of his neck. "I think the whole family would benefit. James and Ann argued the entire time we were gone. Poor Kendall remained silent and morose. I hope they'll be able to adapt, but honestly, I don't have high hopes."

5

———

Emory worked hard to achieve her position as Chief of the Billings USMS office and some days, she wondered why she had wanted the title so badly. Boring bureaucratic meetings had occupied her entire afternoon, and the job had become far more administrative than action oriented. And though she'd expected much of that, the endless meetings were the bane of her career.

Often when Dirk and Hank left the office, she envied them. Even today, when they hadn't relished the idea of meeting with the new family in WITSEC, she would have gladly changed places with them. At least Dirk didn't have to face the subtext and innuendo she did regarding their relationship. If he attended the same meetings, their peers wouldn't dare give him the flack she received.

She unlocked the door to her apartment and went inside, dropping her bags on a bench in the hallway and kicking off her shoes. She dug through her purse to find her phone and typed out a message to Dirk.

Emory: **Hey, free for dinner?**

Emory flung herself onto the sofa and rubbed her sore feet while she waited for his answer.

Dirk: **What do u have in mind?**

Emory: **Lasagna, a beefy Cabernet, and...**

Dirk: **Def in for the "and..." What time?**

Emory laughed. At least in that realm of their relationship, Dirk was predictable. Her thumb tapped the screen.

Emory: **Say 6?**

Dirk: **Still getting the family settled. Then I gotta drop Hank off at my house. Can we shoot for 6:30 - 7?**

Emory: **Sure. See u then.**

Dirk let himself into her apartment just before 7:00. "Honey, I'm home! God, it smells amazing in here."

Emory came out of the kitchen carrying her wine. "Hey, how was your day?"

Dirk took the glass from her, drank a large sip, and set it on the bar that separated the kitchen from the dining room. He gathered her in his arms. "Long." He kissed her intensely enough to leave her breathless. "Yours?"

"Also long. And boring. How are the Millers settling in?"

"Not well. The dad is arrogant and angry, the mom is hysterical. Kendall, the witness, is an emotional mess, and the middle son is even angrier than his dad. The only one who might do well is the littlest kid, Joey."

"They just need time to adjust."

"Maybe, but I'm not holding my breath."

Emory clasped his hand and pulled him behind her.

"Come on. Let me get you a glass of your own wine. Dinner is about ready."

Over the cheesy Italian dish, Dirk told her all about his day, and she filled him in on hers. Side by side, they cleaned up from their meal and took their refilled glasses to the living room. "Enough about work. I want to talk about Thanksgiving."

Dirk grimaced and rested his head back on the couch. "How many did you say are going to be coming?"

"You, me, Hank, and maybe Amy, Teresa and Tomas, and my parents. Oh—and I thought I'd invite Laurie and Caleb, too."

Dirk's tone took on an edge. "How do you see this going between me and your dad? Is he expecting me to ask for your hand? The whole day will be incredibly awkward if he is."

His mood change frustrated her. "Don't be like that. He knows you're important to me, and so he wants to meet you. That's all."

"Except we don't know if we have a future together or not, so what am I supposed to say to him?"

His words cut her to the quick, and she choked on her wine. "What?"

"You know what I mean. What we have going is great, but ultimately, you and I don't want the same things out of life. The time will come when you opt to move on. How do we explain that to the General? He probably expects me to ask some big question, and what am I supposed to say? 'No, Sir. All we want is to sleep together for a while.'"

Emory set her glass down hard enough to splash wine

onto the coffee table. "Is that really how you see our relationship?"

"That's how your dad is going to see it."

"But how do *you* view it, Dirk?"

He sat up and took her hand. "Emory, you know I love you. But you dream of having kids, the white picket fence, the whole deal. And you know I don't. Honestly, I think you'll eventually decide you need to follow your dreams. And you should. I want you to have everything you desire. I do. But *I'm* not the guy to give it to you."

Emory's throat constricted, and the ache made tears form in her eyes. "I guess it's good to know how you see our future. Don't you have any room for options?"

"What options?"

"Well, for one thing, I could decide I'd rather be with you—and not have kids—than to lose what we have. Also, does it ever occur to you how great you are with children? Look at the relationships you have with Caleb and Tomas. You'd be such an incredible dad. Maybe you'll change your mind?"

Dirk sighed and ran his hand over his face. "Emory, you can't hold on to that hope. I've been as honest as I can with you. I've been there, and done that, and I'm not going through it again."

"I know you're scared, Dirk. I can't begin to imagine what losing Bennett was like for you. But that kind of thing isn't likely to happen again." Emory pictured a young Dirk not only suffering under the incredible grief after the death of his precious son, but from the added pain of discovering his wife in bed with his best friend. Betrayed by the two people he needed most.

He shook his head. "Besides, most families I know are miserable. Look at Hank and Amy. The Millers are another great example of familial bliss. Laurie lost Sam, and now she and Caleb are on their own. Even my friend Caitlyn and her husband Colt are struggling. The job isn't good for families and—"

Emory reached for him. "And you don't want to risk hurting like you did when Bennett died. I understand that, Dirk, but maybe the love we have is worth the risk."

Angry tears flashed in his obsidian eyes. He shot to his feet and strode to the balcony's sliding door. He stared out at the night, keeping his back to her. "Maybe for you, but not for me."

She followed him and slid her arms around his waist, pressing her cheek against his shoulder blade. "Okay, then. We can discuss not having children." Her voice caught on the words. "But don't dismiss me from your future. I love you, Dirk, and I want to be with you."

Dirk's muscles flexed, but he said nothing in return.

6

Volodymyr Kovalenko sat at his usual chrome and gray-flecked Formica table at the back of Pierogi Hastronom, the local Ukrainian deli where he often held court during the day. Folk music from the old country streamed softly from speakers set in the restaurant's ceiling. He sipped thick, dark coffee as he gazed beyond the shoulder of the man who sat facing him. Mishka Fomichev was Volodymyr's right-hand man, his Kapitan, and the Kovalenko Family attorney. Volodymyr's focus, however, was internal, though he kept his features placid, belying the fury within.

"You know, Mishka, I came to the United States from nothing. I would have died unnoticed in the back alleys of Odessa if the wife of Burian Hordiyenko hadn't adopted me." Hordiyenko was the head of the entire family business whose headquarters remained in Brighton Beach. "Burian raised me up as his own son, taught me the family business, and honored me with the leadership of my own region here in New Jersey."

Volodymyr's gaze blurred as he sifted through old memories. The most powerful among them went as far back as he could remember when he was a child, starving in Ukraine. He had vague images of a woman who must have been his mother. She cared for him when he was small, but for a reason unknown to him, she disappeared. When Volodymyr was only five, he ended up living on the streets, scrounging from other beggars who took pity on him. He had been cold, filthy, and starving when a woman he didn't know put him in her car and drove him away from the squalor he was scraping his existence from. Volodymyr didn't know where she was taking him, but he remembered the relief he felt at the heat blowing on him from the vents in the vehicle's dashboard.

They had ended up at a tall gray-stone building. The woman took his hand and led him up the steps and inside. He followed her into an office where a woman who wore her black hair slicked back into a tight bun at the back of her head sat at a wooden desk. She terrified him, and he couldn't look her in the eye. The women spoke a long while, and he fidgeted with the need to pee. He had tried his best to hold it, but eventually his body won out, and he wet his pants.

The woman next to him jumped to the side. "Oh dear! Call the janitor!"

Volodymyr remembered vividly the depth of his fear and shame as he stared at the puddle forming around his worn, too-small shoes. Tears dripped from his eyes, and he bit his lip hard to keep from crying out loud.

Behind the desk, the severe woman stood and assessed the situation. "I see we have been too long with this interview." She came around her desk, and standing before him, the woman touched his chin and lifted his face. When he looked up at her, he expected anger and disgust, but surprisingly, she gazed down at him with kind eyes. "What is your name, *malyatko?*" She used the word of endearment his mother had often called him that meant "little one".

"Volodymyr," he murmured. It had been days since he had spoken aloud, and his voice sounded like burlap.

"A fine, strong name. I am *Micic* Petrenco. I am the head matron here at the Ukrainian Children's Charity Home." She smiled, and his shoulders relaxed. "I will send you with *Micic* Rybak. She will help you bathe and give you clean clothes to wear. You'll be staying here with us until we can find a family for you. How does that sound?"

Volodymyr hadn't understood what she meant. Not really. But he stared up at her and trusted the large dark eyes that beamed down at him, so he nodded.

"Very well."

A plump older woman entered the room. Her gray eyebrows rose to touch the brim of the white cap pinned to her hair. "Well, now. Who do we have here?" *Micic* Petrenko explained, and the older lady cooed. "Alright, then Master Volodymyr. My name is *Micic* Rybak. Come with me, and I'll get you cleaned up and settled." She took his hand, paying no attention to the dirt smudges and dingy fingernails, and marched him off to a bathroom that had many sinks, toilets, and several bathtubs.

His memories of the orphanage were warm. He remembered his belly finally feeling full and having clean clothes to wear. *Micic* Rybak was both mother and teacher to the group of boys in the dorm room. There were girls in the orphan asylum too, but they lived on the other side of the building.

Volodymyr lived there for two years before one morning *Micic* Petrenco called him into her office. "I have wonderful news for you, Volod! A man and his wife who live in New York want to adopt you!"

Volodymyr met the news with great fear. He didn't want to leave his family at the orphanage to live with strangers, and he had no idea where New York was.

Micic Petrenco realized his trepidation and rushed around her desk to embrace him. "Dear, Volod. This is good news! I promise you. Have you ever heard of the United States of America?" She showed him where Ukraine was on the globe that sat on her desk and then spun the orb and pointed to a distant land across the ocean. "America is where all your dreams can come true. *Pan* and *Micic* Hordiyenko live here," she pointed to the edge of the land near the water, "in New York City. They want you to be their son, Volod! You are very lucky. *Pan* Hordiyenko is a very important man."

Volodymyr had not known how truly important Burian Hordiyenko was. Not until he was fourteen, and he was first invited to sit in on the meetings his adoptive father held in the vast library of his grand home. Not until he watched as a battered man who owed his father money begged from his knees for Burian's mercy, tears and snot streaming together on his face. Not until Burian offered the beggar a bullet in place of the understanding the man sought.

Micic Petrenco had been correct when she told him how he was lucky to be adopted by the Hordiyenkos. After his arrival in the United States, the Hordiyenkos provided Volodymyr with everything he needed and more. After proving himself loyal to the Hordiyenko family by working up through the ranks and becoming a made man, they afforded him an education from Columbia University.

Volodymyr never forgot the cold and treacherous streets from which he came. He owed his adoptive parents everything. Volodymyr worked hard to graduate with honors and his father awarded him with his own branch of the family business. Burian even set Volod up in his own mansion in Deal, New Jersey.

That was forty years ago, and he had built his own empire since then. An empire whose security was now threatened by a mere teenage girl. He couldn't bear the look of disgust and disappointment he knew he'd see in Burian's eyes if he allowed this screw-up to bring the Hordiyenko family down.

Mishka's voice snapped him out of his memories. "You've done yourself proud, Volod. And your gifts to the Ukrainian Children's Charity are beyond generous."

Volodymyr snapped his eyes back to Fomichev's face. "Until now. This blunder could undermine the entire family. If that Bennington girl identifies either Andriy or Pavlo, my branch of the family is finished." He gripped the sides of the Formica-topped table. "We must stop that from happening."

A server hesitantly approached their table. "Excuse my interruption, Mr. Kovalenko, but I have your

Yabluchnyk." He set two plates of warm Ukrainian apple cake before the men and bowed as he backed away from them.

Volodymyr and Mishka savored their first cinnamon-sugar-flavored bites before Mishka glanced around him for eavesdroppers. Finding none, he responded, "Unfortunately, we are still unable to find any trail of the Bennington family. We must face the possibility that they are in witness protection. We may never locate them."

"Unacceptable!" Volodymyr shouted, causing other patrons at the deli to turn and stare. He lowered his voice and leaned forward. "Tell the men they *must* find the girl. Not only do I face humiliation before the family, but the FBI and the Attorney General claim they have enough evidence to freeze my bank accounts."

"What kind of evidence? You weren't at the scene of the crime. How are they connecting you to any of this?"

"It's that idiot, Pavlo. The night of the mission, he used his prized possession during the job."

Mishka's bushy salt and pepper brows crunched together into a dark, fuzzy questioning line.

Volodymyr explained, "He owns a silenced Makarov PB pistol given to him by his father. They are rare and uniquely Ukrainian. He did not retrieve all his shell casings from the Davis home before he and Andriy left. This fact alone caused the eyes of the FBI to turn toward our family. Pavlo's father bought the gun at a public arms show and registered the weapon under Pavlo's name."

"Have they arrested him? I haven't been called to the jail."

"No. He's in hiding, for now. But I don't know how long I can protect him."

"All our men are out searching for leads, but it's as though one day the Bennington family lived in Ridgefield, and the next, they were simply gone. Their house is up for sale, but the listing agent claims the seller is anonymous. All she has is a bank account and electronic signatures."

"That's it!" Volodymyr skidded his chair backward in a surge of excitement. "The realtor must have an email address. Get that and we can find the Benningtons' IP address."

Fomichev's shoulders rounded forward, and he sighed. "We have already tried that. But the IP address leads us to the US Marshal's office in New Haven. It's a dead end."

"If the US Marshals are involved, we can be certain they are hiding the family until the trial. Our only chance to locate them is to lean on old acquaintances or work colleagues the Benningtons might contact."

"Yes, sir. But we have another hope, and I think a better one, which is to monitor the social media accounts of the two older Bennington kids. They're less likely to be cautious and could inadvertently give us clues to where they are hiding."

"Very good thinking. Are you on that?"

"Yes, sir. We've created a false profile of a beautiful young girl who will seek to connect with friends of Melissa Bennington's old boyfriend. Gradually, our pretend girl will ask to be his friend. I'm hoping we can get them talking and flirting to make Melissa jealous. A scorned teenage girl is likely to respond in some way. And as soon as she does, we can reel her in. I think it's our best shot."

"Fine. But we have no time to waste. Find her, Mishka, before you and I end up poor and in prison, or more likely dead, after Burian Hordiyenko puts out a hit on us."

"He wouldn't..."

"He would. And frankly, I couldn't blame him. He enjoys the power he does because he is ruthless. And as soon as we eliminate Melissa Bennington, I will do the same to Andriy and Pavlo. I must make examples out of them."

Fomichev swallowed, and rubbing his chin, he nodded. The benefits of belonging in the top ranks of the family were great, but so was the risk of disappearing at the whim of the boss.

7

____

Melissa stared at her reflection in the mirror and pushed a long, silky brown swath of hair behind her ear. She spoke her new name out loud to the face glowering back at her. "Kendall." She pasted on a smile. "Hi! I'm Kendall!" Her voice squeaked. Too much enthusiasm. "I'm Kendall. What's your name?" Groaning, she spun away from the glass and stomped to her bed. She hated being the new kid. It was the worst!

"Kendall!" the disembodied voice of her mother called from down the hall. "Breakfast is ready!"

Her mom tried to act as though everything was normal. She did her best to make sure all the kids felt safe and secure in their insane situation. Which would never happen. All Kendall could think about was the shooting and how she missed her friends in Connecticut like lost limbs—both the ones who were living and the ones who had been killed. Her heart clenched into a fist at the memory of her closest friends with blood flowing from holes in their bodies and the terrifying men who shot them. Their faces seared themselves into her brain. She would never forget, and she would make them pay for what they did.

"Be there in a minute." Kendall yelled back. She grabbed her phone and opened the Instagram app she downloaded with her new profile. The marshals told them to stay off social media, but who were they kidding? There was no way she would not spy on her friends from back home. Besides, she wasn't stupid. She uploaded a cat emoji for her profile picture and used her new fake name. No one would ever know it was her.

Kendall searched for her boyfriend Fletcher's profile. If she just looked but didn't follow him, no one could tell she was stalking her old life. Fletch's profile picture lit her screen, and her chest ached with loss. She missed him desperately. If only she could reach out, maybe they could have a secret romance until she was eighteen. By then, the killers would be in jail and she and Fletcher could pick up where they left off.

She scrolled down through photos of the funerals of her friends. Tears pooled and spilled over her eyelids, ruining her mascara and makeup job. Guilt choked her sobs. They should have killed her, too. Why was her life spared? Why was she still alive but torn away from the life she knew? If she had died that night, her dad wouldn't have had to change careers and Easton... *Jack...* Would she ever get used to calling her brothers by different names? *Jack* should have been on his way to a college baseball scholarship. All because of her, his life plans were in ruins.

"Kendall!"

"Coming!" Kendall patted her cheeks with a tissue, hoping to fix the damage. She dusted her face with powder and reapplied black to her lashes. She shrugged at her reflection. *Well, here goes.* She opened her bedroom door to the alluring scent of bacon, which she followed down the hall to the small kitchen.

"Good morning, sweetheart. You look cute today."

"Thanks, Mom." Kendall pulled out a chair from the kitchen table. Her mom set a plate stacked high with chocolate chip pancakes and bacon.

"Do you want milk or OJ?" Her mom wore an apron like Betty Crocker or someone. *Must be part of her new persona.*

"Milk." Kendall sat down, glancing at her brothers, who were both face down in their plates. "Where's Dad?"

Her mom set a glass of milk before her. "He's getting dressed. He has three job interviews today."

"I can't believe the cops didn't just set him up with a job like they did us with school. How awkward for him to have to beg for work." Kendall's dad had been an extremely successful investment banker in their old life. None of them wanted for anything. The kitchen in their Connecticut home was bigger than their entire new house altogether. This whole thing was humiliating.

"It's more authentic this way. No reason for anyone to be suspicious. He won't have a problem getting hired, I'm sure."

Kendall shoved a bite of syrupy cakes into her mouth before she could say anything she'd regret. Her mom only wanted to help, even if she was trying *way* too hard. Life sucked. A fake smile, an apron, and a pile of pancakes couldn't change that.

Her mom flipped more cakes and returned to the table. "I'll take Joey to school today and get him signed in, but starting tomorrow, you two older kids can drop him off on your way. Okay?"

Jack ignored their mother, but Kendall nodded. Their father entered the room dressed in an ill-fitting suit. Kendall did a double take. She was used to seeing him styled in fine wool and linen jackets tailored to fit his frame. If she were honest, she'd say he looked frumpy. Just the way she imagined some old corporate accountant would look.

She smiled at him. "You look sharp, Dad. You're going to kill it today."

He rolled his eyes and poured himself a cup of coffee. Kendall's mother said nothing, not even to offer her dad breakfast. The tension between her parents was awful. And that was her fault, too. Kendall's upcoming testimony caused them all to lose the comfortable lives they were used to, and she didn't know how to fix it. Whenever she said anything to her mom and dad, it only made things worse. So, she stuffed another bite into her mouth.

Skipping breakfast, her dad kissed her cheek, patted Jack on the shoulder and mussed Joey's hair. "Wish me luck," he said with no enthusiasm.

"Bye, Dad! You'll do great!" Kendall's tone was that of a cheerleader—way too excited—and her encouragement lay like a dead thing on the floor. She slumped in her chair.

On their way to school, Kendall and Jack remained quiet and inside their own thoughts until Kendall finally garnered the courage to broach the elephant that walked between them. "I'm really sorry about all of this, Jack. I wish—"

"It's fine, Kendall. It's better than you being dead." His tone was less than convincing.

She sighed and tucked her chin. After another block, she asked, "Do we have any classes together?" She pulled up a screenshot of her schedule on her phone.

"Doubt it." Jack didn't bother to look.

Kendall swiped to a map of the school, hoping to pre-determine where her first class of the day was. "I have English Comp first hour. How about you?"

"Geometry."

"Yuck. First thing? That's brutal."

That got a slight grin from him. "Not when you're a math genius like me and Dad."

"True. You guys are such nerds!" They laughed, and though it was stiff, it was a start. After a few minutes, she spoke again. "Look, Jack. I realize I should have just kept my mouth shut. If I never told anyone about seeing what I saw, our lives would still be the same. I'm really sorry."

Jack stopped and turned toward her. He hitched his backpack up higher on his shoulders. "You know that's not true. You had to call 911. And besides, those types of guys aren't the kind to wait and see if you're going to iden-tify them. They would have found you and... well, they probably would have taken our whole family out. We had to do this. It just sucks. That's all."

Sliding his arm around her shoulders, he stepped off again. "I think we have the same lunch period—thank God. I hate being the new kid, but it's worse if you have to sit by yourself in the cafeteria."

8

Joey's mom insisted on kissing him goodbye as they stood next to the flagpole in front of his new elementary school, and he figured now all the kids thought he was a total baby.

"Have a great day, Punkin!" She squeezed him tight. Could this get any worse?

His shoulders eased with relief at the sound of the morning bell. "Got to go, Mom." Joey pulled away from her grasp.

"Okay. Come home right after school. I'll want to hear all about your first day." His mom stood waving her fluffy cream-mittened hand. She looked like she was ready to go to one of her charity meetings with earmuffs over her smooth brown hair that matched her mittens and UGGs. Why couldn't she stay in the car like the other moms who hid behind their giant sunglasses and sipped coffee from thermal mugs? His mom always drew attention. He'd hear about it later out on the playground... he was pretty sure.

Joey raised his hand in a half-hearted wave and plodded toward the red brick building, thankful his mom decided she didn't need to come in with him. Inside, he found the office and stood by the reception desk. No one paid any attention to him. He moved to one of three chairs that lined the wall next to the principal's office and waited.

The second bell rang, and the halls grew quiet. Joey sat through the morning announcement and finally a chubby lady wearing what looked like a dressy sweatsuit walked past him, stopped, and took two steps back.

"Who do we have here?" Her smile was friendly, and Joey sat up.

"I'm Ash—I mean, um, I'm Joey Miller."

"Oh, yes! The new boy. My name is Mrs. Oglesthorpe. I'm the Office Administrator here." She laughed. "I know... my name is a mouthful. Don't worry, everyone just calls me Mrs. 'O'. I forgot today is the day you start school here." She grinned at him and spread her arms wide. "Welcome to Big Horn Elementary, Joey. Let's get you to your classroom. Your teacher is Mrs. Tyree. All the kids love her."

Mrs. 'O' turned on her heel and marched out of the office, heading left down the main hall that smelled like paste. Joey grabbed his pack and scrambled to follow her. The hallways were dark, not like his old school that had tons of windows. He counted the doors they passed so he'd be able to find his classroom tomorrow on his own.

The lady opened the door to a noisy room at the end of the hall and pushed him ahead of her as they entered. His tummy hurt like the time his brother threw a football at him, and it hit him in the guts. A thin woman with light-brown hair, wearing a blue dress that looked like a long shirt, stood at the front of the class. She stopped talking and turned to them as they walked in. All the kids got quiet and stared.

"Mrs. Tyree, this is Joey Miller. He's new to Big Horn and will join your class."

His new teacher's eyes shone when she smiled, and he relaxed. "Hello, Joey. We've been expecting you. You're going to fit right in. Please hang your backpack on a peg above the cubbies and sit at the open desk in the second row." Mrs. Tyree nodded to Mrs. 'O'. "Thank you, Betsy."

Joey hung his pack on a hook and slid into his chair. Mrs. Tyree had printed his name on a rectangular piece of paper taped to his desk. His breath came easier. His teacher really was expecting him.

The room had windows all along one wall with plants sitting in the sun on the counter. His teacher posted alphabet cards across the top of the board, and there was a bulletin board decorated for Thanksgiving next to it. He crossed his arms on his desk and rested his chin on them as he watched Mrs. Tyree write numbers on the whiteboard.

"We're learning how to multiply, Joey. Did you learn this yet in your old school, or is this new for you?"

Joey sat up, not expecting her to talk to him. "Uh... yeah. I mean, I... we were starting to learn it at Holcombe." He winced when he said the name of his old school out loud. Deputy Hank told him he must not tell anyone the names of places where he lived before.

Mrs. Tyree didn't seem to notice. "That's great! Bear

with us if any of this is old news to you. We'll all be on the same page in no time. Everyone, take out a piece of paper and a pencil. I want you to copy down all the multiples of two."

After math came reading. Mrs. Tyree had the kids pass a book around the room. Everybody had to read a paragraph out loud. Joey always hated this part of third grade. But he lucked out when the recess bell rang before it was his turn. He followed all the kids as they ran to get their coats and line up at the classroom door.

A kid with black hair stood behind him and tapped his back. "Hey, wanna play on the swings?"

Joey looked over his shoulder at the boy. "Yeah, sure."

"I'm Tomas."

"I'm Joey."

"I know."

Mrs. Tyree opened the door and released her class. Once they were outside, Tomas pointed out the swing set and the two boys took off across the playground to claim their seat. Joey climbed onto the flexible rubber strip next to his new friend, but another, bigger kid, grabbed the chain before he could push off.

"Hey Joey, dude, you don't want to be friends with Tomas. He's not even a real American."

Tomas stood up, and curling his fists, he took a step toward the new kid. "Shut up, Brett. I am too! Come on, Joey. Let's go."

Joey looked between Tomas and the tall kid with freckles and sand-colored hair flanked by three of his friends. One boy stuck his foot out behind Tomas and pushed him, causing him to trip and fall to the ground. A group of girls from their class watched them from the four-square court. They giggled when Brett tossed his long bangs and smiled at them. Joey's chest was tight. He wanted to help Tomas up, but then he thought it might go better for him if he made friends with this gang.

Tomas got to his feet, brushed dirt from his hands and walked away, looking back to see if Joey was following him. Joey's belly felt like he'd swallowed a bucket full of rocks, but he remained on the swing. The dark-haired boy, who was almost Joey's first friend, shook his head, and with his shoulders hunched, he left Joey to play with the new group of boys.

"Smart move, Miller." Brett slapped his back. "Let's go play kick ball!" Joey ran with the band of boys to a chain-link backstop on the far end of the playground.

After school, Brett asked Joey to walk home with his buddies and him, but Joey explained that his brother and sister were picking him up.

"Too bad, cuz we're going to stop by 7-11 on the way. The man who works there, Mr. Grant, sometimes gives us candy when we go in."

"Cool! I can probably walk home with you guys tomorrow. Just since it's my first day, my mom is being all strict and everything."

"Yeah, maybe. You're missing out, dude. He'll probably give us all the candy today and there won't be any left tomorrow."

Joey's stomach growled. He was hungry, and the candy sure sounded good. "I wish I could go with you today, but..."

"Your loss, dude." Brett shrugged on his coat and

called to his crew with a toss of his bangs. Joey watched the group leave together.

Tomas approached and stood next to him, watching, too. "Those guys aren't good kids. But do what you want. I gotta go to after-school care."

It made Joey feel worse that Tomas was still willing to talk to him after he ditched him on the playground. He opened his mouth to say he was sorry, but Tomas was already walking down the hall toward the gym.

Joey hated being the new kid.

9

That afternoon, after Dirk and Hank brought their cyber-hunt for fugitives to an end, they drove out to check on the Miller family. Dirk drove, and they arrived at the house before school was out, hoping to speak with James and Ann Miller before their kids got home. Together, the partners approached the door. Yelling and a crash that sounded like breaking glass greeted them before they got to the front door.

"What was that?" Hank reached for his weapon, holding it at low ready as they stepped onto the porch.

Dirk sighed. The scene was all too familiar to him. He remembered the fights he and his ex, Hannah, got into before they finally split. Not bothering to unholster his gun, Dirk knocked on the door. The angry sounds ceased, immediately followed by hurried footfalls and murmurs Dirk couldn't make out.

Ann opened the door, but only as wide as her face. She peered out. "Oh, Deputies..." She swung the door open fully. "Come in. Is everything alright? It's not one of the kids, is it?" Sudden fear cast shadows in her eyes.

"No, ma'am. Hank and I just stopped by to check in. We wanted to see how things are going, and if you need anything."

Ever the upper-crust lady, Ann stepped aside and gestured them toward the tiny living/family room. "Please, come in. Have a seat. Can I offer you something to drink?"

Dirk smirked to himself. Her polished manners stood out in the western town of Billings, Montana. But she could explain them away simply by saying she came from back east. "No, thank you. Why don't you and James sit down with us for a minute?"

"Oh. Yes. Of course." Ann's eyes hardened when she cast her gaze at her husband, who was in the kitchen sweeping up some remaining slivers of glass. "James?"

Dirk waited for James to dump the dustpan in the trash and join them. "There's no benefit in acting like you two weren't having an argument a few minutes ago. Instead of pretending, I want to encourage you. Changing a family's entire identity is incredibly stressful, but with help, you can be successful. We'd like to suggest, again, that you meet with the USMS therapist. She can help you through the rough spots." He turned toward James. "You had some job interviews today. How did that go?"

James slumped in his chair. "Not good. And I have to tell you, this whole thing is insulting. I could out account any of those accountants. Maybe I'm too confident for their liking. Who knows why none of the firms offered me a job? They would if I could put my true credentials down on my resume. I don't know how to go from the thrill of making massive million-dollar deals and trades and enjoying the incredible income that came with it, to the dreary backroom of some mediocre accounting firm in the middle of nowhere, USA, for minimum wage."

"Oh, for God's sake. You won't be making minimum wage!" Ann crossed her arms over her chest and glared at her husband. "I'm so tired of listening to you whine. You're just mad that you actually have to work for a living now and can't fill your days with long lunches with the secretarial pool."

The front door opened, and the three Miller kids walked in. From his own experience of standing on the other side of the thin entry door, Dirk was certain the kids heard the angry words of their parents. Kendall glared at them with tears trembling on her lower lids. Jack rolled his eyes, snatched up a basketball that sat by the door, and left. Joey simply stared at the adults in the room. "Dad, you used to have lunch at a pool with secretaries?"

Hank's hand shot up to cover his grin. When he composed himself, he stood. "Come on, Joey. Let's go shoot hoops with Jack and let the grown-ups talk." Together, they went outside.

"Dad?" Kendall's shocked expression searched her father's defensive one.

James jumped to his feet. "Your mother is just spouting off, princess."

"Sure, whatever." Ann crossed her legs and turned her back to James.

Dirk didn't doubt her veiled claim that James had

been dallying with other women when he was in the city at his firm on Wall Street. But maybe this common challenge would eventually bring them together. He gave himself an internal scoff. *Yeah, right.* He didn't hold out a lot of faith in a broken marriage mending itself back together.

James sat on the arm of the couch. "What about you, Sterling? You married?"

"No." His interior armor closed ranks. He wasn't about to share his life with these people.

"Well, it isn't easy. Let me tell you. No matter how hard you work, no matter how much money you make, no matter what fancy things you buy for your wife, she's never happy."

Kendall groaned and tromped down the hall to her bedroom, slamming the door behind her.

"Look," Dirk leaned forward, propping his forearms on his knees. "You two have to hold it together for your kids' sake. I know it's hard. This is maybe the most difficult thing you will ever do, but you're alive and you're together. Try to focus on that. See the therapist. Start over. Whatever it takes, but don't lose sight of the few years you have to help your kids adjust to their new lives. They're what's important, right?"

Ann glanced down the hall and lowered her voice. "You don't know what it's like to look at the man you married and know he's been sleeping with other women —young, beautiful women—while you're home raising his children. It was one thing when he was never home but supplied a huge income. I could almost ignore what I knew was going on so long as I lived my comfortable suburban life. But here? With James home all the time? Whining and cry-babying about having to work at an actual job? It's just too much."

James glared at his wife. "With the pittance of a salary these firms offer here in Billings, you're going to need to go to work, too, *Ann.* How do you feel about that? Do you even have any marketable skills? I doubt experience as the PTA president will get you very far."

Dirk noticed James didn't deny his wife's accusation, and he held up a hand to stop their bickering. "None of this is helpful right now." He passed a business card to Ann with the name of the therapist. "In case you lost her number. Call her. She can help. On the practical side of things, do you need anything? James, would it help if my boss reached out to one of the accounting firms you're applying to, to grease the skids?"

James sighed. "I don't need any help. I can get a job. I'll go back out tomorrow."

"Okay, I'm going to check on Kendall." Dirk's heart broke for the kids in this messed up family, though he didn't know what more he could do for them than listen.

10

Hank shivered as an early winter breeze cut through his jacket and rustled the brown leaves gathered in the street gutters. The air smelled like snow. There were only a few days left of the dwindling autumn. He zipped the front of his coat closed. "Are you warm enough, Joey?"

The kid looked at him like he was crazy and took off, coatless, toward the basketball court where Jack practiced free throws before an audience of three admiring girls. Hank chuckled, remembering never feeling cold as a kid. He also remembered how it felt when girls first started noticing him like was happening with Jack. Times were much simpler back then. Thoughts of Amy skimmed through his mind, but he pushed them away. The struggles he and his wife were having had nothing to do with the Miller boys. He jogged to catch up with Joey.

"East—" Joey caught himself calling his brother by his old name. He glanced guiltily over his shoulder at Hank and then shouted again. "Jack! Let me have a turn!"

Jack took another shot, and one of the girls who stood just beyond the basket caught the ball after it swished through the net. "Nice shot." She smiled and bounce-passed it back to him.

"Hey, Miller!" One of five boys playing football on the field below the court called to him. "Come play ball. You'd round the teams out to three on both sides."

Jack responded to the girl by grinning at his shoes, then rolled the basketball to Joey. "Go for it, kid. I'm gonna play football." He jogged down the hill to the field, and the girls followed to watch the impromptu game.

Joey sighed out his disappointment. "Will *you* play HORSE with me, Hank?"

"Sure, buddy. You take the first shot."

After several rounds of shooting for baskets and missing for Joey's sake, Hank saw the older boys taking a break. They went to sit with the girls on the side of the hill and relived the best parts of their game, laughing and teasing each other in the way of boys.

"Jack, dude. You can really throw the ball. Were you in sports at your last school?"

"Nah."

"It sucks it's too late for you to go out for our team this year. You're way better than Sanders. He's the quarterback. What sports do you play? The basketball team is already practicing, so it's probably too late for that, but what about baseball in the spring?"

"Yeah! Tommy plays right field and pitcher. Right, Tommy?" another boy chimed in.

Tommy picked up the theme. "Yeah, Miller. With your arm, I bet you'd be great at baseball. Can you hit?"

Jack sent a hateful glance toward Hank. Poor kid. Hank got it. And he hoped Jack could field the earnest questions of his new friends. There was no way to hide his natural abilities, and this conversation had to sting. "Man, the timing of our move really sucked. I'll go out for football next year, though."

"Nice!" The boys accepted his answer at face value and moved on to other topics, but the girl who had passed him the basketball leaned toward him.

"I'm freshman cheer captain. It would be super fun to cheer for you, Jack." Her cheeks pinkened, and she turned to her friends. "Right?" The threesome giggled together.

Obviously uncomfortable with the attention, Jack held his hands up for Tommy to toss him the ball. "Come on, guys. We have a second half to play."

Relieved that Jack was able to distract the kids' curiosity about him, Hank helped Joey practice his dribbling. "How was your first at school, Joey?"

"Pretty good." The ball hit Joey's toe and bounced away. He chased it and returned to try again. "I made some new friends. They asked me to go to 7-11 with them after school. They said they go there a lot cuz sometimes the owner gives them candy." Joey held the ball and looked up at Hank. "Can I go with them sometime?"

"Sounds like fun, but you'll have to ask your mom and dad, kiddo. That's one thing that hasn't changed."

"How come my mom and dad yell at each other all the time?"

Hank's chest squeezed. "Your family has gone

through a lot of hard stuff lately, and that's difficult for everybody, especially grown-ups."

"It is?" Joey squinted at him.

"Yep. Be patient with them. Everything will work out eventually."

"I'm cold."

"Me too. Let's go back to your house. Besides, you never got an after-school snack."

Joey's eyes rounded. "Yeah!" He took off toward home.

Hank hoped Dirk had enough time to get things under control while they were gone because a hungry eight-year-old was about to blast through the front door.

11

———

Emory sat at her desk sipping her Earl Grey tea, breathing in the fragrant citrusy bergamot steam. She very much needed the caffeine boost it would give her to get through the rest of the day. She and Teresa had been working heads down at their desks all afternoon. A smile curled her lips when she heard the bell announcing the elevator arriving on their floor.

She had expected Dirk and Henry to return to the office at any moment. Dirk's teasing and Henry's responding laughter echoed down the hall. The tenor of Dirk's deep voice sent both a thrill and a sense of apprehension coursing through her blood. Emory stood, straightened her skirt, and ran a quick hand over her hair to smooth any stray strands. Looking for a reason to come out of her office, she drained her teacup and headed toward the break room to make more.

Henry was the first one through the office door. "Hey, Teresa. What's up? Chief?"

Teresa tossed her long black braid over her shoulder, sat back in her chair, and turned to face the men. "Not much. Just catching up on paperwork."

Dirk's eyes sought Emory's, and the ghost of a smile passed across his mouth before he turned his attention to their admin. "It's about quitting time, T. What are you and Tomas up to tonight?"

"The usual. Pick him up from school, drive home, scrounge around for something for dinner, supervise homework, and go to bed."

"Sounds about right." Dirk's gaze returned to Emory. "Do we have enough time to debrief our day? Or would you rather do it during the morning meeting tomorrow?"

"Do you have something urgent to report? Is the Miller family settling in all right?" Emory blew the steam away from her fresh tea.

Dirk slid out of his leather jacket and tossed it on the back of his chair. "There's not much new to report other than the family seems unstable. When Hank and I arrived at the house this afternoon, the parents were fighting. We tried to deescalate the situation, but it didn't happen before the kids came home from school. Hank went with the boys over to the park, but Kendall got upset and locked herself in her room. James Miller is extremely unsatisfied with the future of his new career, and his wife is equally unhappy with him. There's a lot of blame being thrown around. Honestly, I don't know if they're going to make it."

Emory's heart softened at the concern written across Dirk's face. He cared more about the Millers than he liked to admit. "It's important for us to remain detached from the family on some level. A lot of broken families enter WITSEC or break after the stress. In fact, that shouldn't surprise us."

Henry sat on the corner of his desk. "What if they can't keep it together, Chief? Do people get divorced when they're in WITSEC? I mean, how does that work?"

Emory's fresh tea burned her tongue when she sipped it, and she breathed in cool air over the sting. "Unfortunately, it happens fairly often. It's a challenge, because we have to re-place one parent and that means never seeing each other or, in this case, the kids again, at least until the children are eighteen. There's no shared custody, etcetera. These kinds of decisions, which are difficult in a normal situation, become far more challenging and permanent."

Henry seemed to digest the information, but Dirk shook his head in disgust. "I gave them Janelle Longworth's business card and explained that she was a USMS approved therapist. I hope for the kids' sake the adults can figure out their crap."

"That's good," Emory crossed the room to her office and turning to face her team, leaned on the door frame. "And it's about all we can do."

Henry pushed himself off his desk and shoved his hands inside his pants pockets. "Speaking of therapists, I've got to go. Amy and I have an appointment with ours in half an hour."

Emory gave him what she hoped was an encouraging smile. "I'm glad you two are trying to work through your issues. How has Amy been feeling? Your baby's due in April, right?"

"Yeah. I guess she's feeling okay. We don't really talk a lot outside of our counseling sessions." Henry dropped his voice and murmured, "Honestly, I'm not sure we're going to be able to work things out." He snatched up his coat, and holding it by the collar, he tossed it over his shoulder. "See you guys tomorrow."

"Remember, Amy's invited to our Thanksgiving dinner, if you want her there. But, of course, it's totally up to you." Emory's heart broke for her young deputy.

Henry bobbed his head as he left the office.

Teresa tapped a few keys on her keyboard, and her computer monitor went blank. "That's it for me today, too." She swiveled in her chair to face her. "I meant to tell you, I think Tomas met the Miller boy. Sounds like they're in the same class."

It excited Emory to hear this, but she maintained a mild expression. "What did Tomas have to say about him?"

"Just that there was a new kid in his class that Tomas tried to make friends with him, but then a boy named Brett Anderson, and his band of bullies stepped in and convinced Joey Miller to play with them, instead." Teresa frowned. "It's hard to teach my son to walk away from those boys when even I secretly want to give each of them a good smack."

Dirk laughed. "They'll figure it out. Some of life's most important lessons are learned on the playground—but only when parents and teachers stay out of it."

"Speaking from experience?" Emory smirked.

"One hundred percent!"

Teresa tidied her desk and gathered her things. "Guess I'll see you guys in the morning."

Dirk raised his chin, acknowledging her comment, and Emory gave her a little wave. She waited until she heard Teresa stepping into the elevator before she spoke. "That leaves the two of us." Emory crossed the room and perched on the edge of Dirk's desk. "Do you have plans tonight?"

"Depends. What do you have in mind?" He leered at her suggestively.

"Be serious, Dirk. I'd like to go to dinner. We need to talk."

"That sounds ominous, and way less fun than what I was thinking."

Emory figured Dirk was using humor as a means to keep her at arm's length. He'd been avoiding the difficult conversation they both knew they needed to have. It was risky because the outcome of their pending discussion would either move them forward in their relationship or end it. She and Dirk loved each other, but they each had different ideas for their future. She wanted to get married and have children with him, and he definitely did not. Emory wasn't sure there was a way through this, but she wanted to find one.

"We need to face the issues standing between us, and then maybe we can talk about the other ideas you have in mind." She smiled and reached for his arm, but he stepped away.

His dark gaze pierced hers. "I'm not sure that's how things will work out." He briefly closed his eyes.

Emory drew a deep breath and set her teacup on the

desk. Standing, she took ahold of his hand. "I want to work things out, Dirk. But one way or another, we need to talk this through. I'm hoping we can come up with a solution."

Dirk brushed a lock of her hair behind her ear before meeting her direct gaze. "I know. I just don't see how."

12

———

irk finally agreed to go to dinner with Emory even though he dreaded having the pending conversation with her. He knew it meant the end of what they had built together. Dirk loved Emory, there was no denying that. But she wanted something from him he could not give. No matter how much he cared for her, he was more self-protective still. He would never again—could never again—risk the depth of grief he endured when he lost his toddler son, Bennett. Dirk couldn't even cope with the day-to-day fear of such a horrible possibility, knowing first-hand the emotional damage the death of a child wreaked on a parent. He certainly would never survive such a loss again.

They drove separate cars and met outside a quiet French restaurant that Emory said she enjoyed. Dirk held the door for her and breathed in her jasmine and rose perfume as she passed him. His heart pinched as he realized she had freshened her scent for him. He wanted to bury his face in her neck and long blonde hair and drown in the floral aroma, but after tonight's conversation, he may never have that opportunity again. Dirk didn't want things to end with Emory, but it wasn't fair for him to string her along. She should find someone else to love, someone who would give her a family.

Dirk held Emory's chair for her as she checked her coat with the hostess and sat. He took the seat opposite her. "This is a nice place. I'm underdressed."

Emory gave him an appreciative smile. "You look perfectly fine to me. Have you never been here before?"

Dirk lifted a large menu board and glanced at the selections. "You know I'm more of a beer and burger guy. But the food looks good. I'm hungry." He wondered if she chose such a quiet, intimate place so he'd be less likely to raise his voice. Smart woman.

"The Chateaubriand is delicious here." The waiter approached and took their wine order. Dirk and Emory waded through stilted small talk until the server returned with their filled glasses. Emory raised hers. "Here's to our future together." Her eyes challenged him.

"Here's to doing what's right for both of us." He tapped the rim of her goblet with his.

Emory took a long drink and bit down on her lower lip before she jumped in. "Dirk, I know you're afraid to become a parent again, and I get it. I understand the profound pain you must have gone through when Bennett died, and I'm deeply sorry that you had to go through that. I never want you to feel as though I'm diminishing the intensity of your grief. But it is a rare thing for parents to lose a child so young."

"It may be rare, but it happened to me. The doctors

said it was sudden infant death syndrome and that they have no actual explanation for why it occurred. What if it's genetic?" He sipped his dry wine, taking a moment to let the ache in his throat subside and to gain control over his emotions. "If something like that happened again because of a flaw in my DNA... I couldn't survive that, Emory. I'm simply not willing to take the chance. You cannot imagine my pain. And I never want you to experience it."

Emory reached across the table and gripped his hand. "Plenty of couples who lost infants have gone on to have more children that were perfectly healthy. Maybe we could talk to a geneticist and find out more about what happened. It likely had nothing to do with you. Couldn't we at least try to learn more?"

Dirk's throat tightened, and he swallowed against its thickening walls. "I can't take the risk, Emory. For your sake, I wish I could. I know how much you want kids, which is why I can't ask you to consider not having them." He pulled his hand away from hers. "I think it would be best for you to find someone else. Someone who shares the same dreams as you. A man who could be a really great dad to your kids." His eyes burned, and he wished they were having this conversation at the end of dinner rather than at the beginning. Or better yet, in the privacy of one of their homes.

"But *you* are the man I love, Dirk. I think we can try to find some kind of solution. Something that will make both of us happy. I don't want any of this with someone else." Emory took a healthy gulp of her wine. The server, taking advantage of the break in their deep conversation, stepped up to the table to take their order. When he left, Emory reached for Dirk again, holding her hand palm up expectantly, her green eyes bright behind brimming tears.

The tightness in Dirk's throat spread to his chest, and he resisted taking Emory's hand. "There is no solution that resolves this difference, Em. I wish there was."

"Give me your hand, Dirk." She stretched her fingers toward him. He let out a defeated breath and laced his fingers with hers. "There are two solutions we haven't discussed. What about adoption? That removes any genetic concerns, right? Dirk, I've watched you with Caleb and Tomas. I know you'd make a wonderful father. And there are plenty of children out there in need of loving parents. What do you think?"

Dirk stared at Emory for what seemed like a long time before their entrees arrived. He looked away, and for several minutes, avoided speaking to her.

Once the server placed their dishes on the table, Emory dipped her head to catch his eye. "So? What do you think about that idea?"

"I thought this was about you wanting to have a baby."

"It's true, I would love to have my own child, but there are other options. Though if genetics are truly your concern, we could choose a donor..."

Dirk dropped his fork on to the china plate. The clatter caused several other restaurant patrons to look in their direction. He retrieved his utensil and leaned forward. "First of all, no way in hell. You think I would agree to you carrying another man's baby and then to raising his child? No. Besides, that doesn't alleviate the risk of losing an infant to some mysterious disease no one can do anything about."

Dirk had no reasonable explanation for the sudden flash of raw jealousy that had grabbed him by the throat at Emory's suggestion of being impregnated by some random man's sperm. The emotion made no sense, not really. Especially not when his solution was for Emory to find another man to love and have kids with. God, all of this caused him to feel sick to his stomach. He set his silverware next to his plate and pushed his chair back. He had lost his appetite.

Emory studied him from across the table. She finished her glass of wine and cleared her throat. "Okay, there is only one other solution I can think of. We get married and choose not to have children."

Dirk thought he felt sick before, but her last words punched him straight in the gut. Selfishly, he wanted to get up and leave the restaurant—to escape this excruciating conversation. Instead, he swallowed hard and stretched his jaw sideways. "I would never ask that of you. I know how much you want children. It wouldn't be fair to you. One day you'd wake up and resent me for that choice." Dirk crushed his molars together and ran his hand down his face. "There's no good way out of this, Emory." He pleaded with her through his eyes to understand how painful this whole situation was for him.

She sat back in her chair, glaring at him. "You don't get to tell me how I will feel in the future. That's not fair. Yes, I want children. I want *your* children. But most importantly, I want you. *You* are my choice." A single tear trickled down her cheek. "Obviously, you don't feel the same way." She lifted her napkin and elegantly blotted her lips before placing the cloth across her full, untouched plate. She pushed back her chair, stood and walked to the host station. Dirk sat frozen in place as he watched her retrieve her coat and leave the restaurant.

A full ten minutes later, he tossed enough cash on the table to cover the bill and numbly walked out into the lonely night.

13

Something banged against the side of the house. Joey woke at the noise and listened for what had caused it. Wind whipped against the bare tree branches of a cottonwood outside his bedroom window. Jack slept soundly, which helped Joey feel better about things. He lay in his bed for what seemed like a hundred hours until his tummy begged him to sneak down the hall to the kitchen for one of the chocolate-chip cookies his mom baked earlier.

He kicked his covers away and rolled off his mattress. He stood over his brother for a few minutes and watched Jack's chest rise and fall. Certain he was asleep, Joey crept to their door, and quiet as he could, opened it a crack wide enough to peek through. The hallway was dark except for a night light his mom had plugged into an outlet near the bathroom. He pulled open the door and slipped through.

On tiptoe, Joey made his way to the small kitchen at the end of the hall. The bulb over the stove was on, but the rest of the house was in shadows. Softy he padded to the cookie jar. This is where it got dangerous. Somehow, no matter where in the house she was, his mom could hear him opening the ceramic lid. She always knew, even in their old home, which was way bigger than this one. He climbed onto the counter so he could lift the lid straight up. The trick was to keep it from clacking on the jar itself.

Victory! Joey pumped his fist in the air before reaching inside and pulling out two chocolate chip peanut butter cookies. Replacing the top was just as hard, but he managed. Maybe Dad was right—you could do anything you want, if you worked at it hard enough. Joey chomped through the first cookie in record time, but quickly realized he then needed a glass of milk. Lucky for him, no one stirred when he opened the refrigerator door. He was getting good at these late-night snacking adventures.

His father's voice sounded from the living room, and Joey almost dropped his glass. But his dad wasn't talking to him. Was somebody with him out there? Joey listened hard but heard only his dad. Curiosity swirled through his body. He downed the rest of his milk and edged his way to the opening of the largest room in the house.

With his phone pressed to his ear, his dad paced in the dark room. He sounded angry, but in a whispering sort of way. "Were you able to transfer the funds to my offshore account?" Joey knew what an account was. He had to put some of his allowance in a savings account at the bank. But was his dad talking about a bank that floated on the water like a ship? "Mindy, it's imperative you get this done before the Feds find the shell companies and freeze the money."

Shell companies? Joey supposed it made sense that companies that sold shells would want to use a bank that floated on the water, but who wanted frozen dollars? He slid down the wall till he sat on the floor and nibbled his second cookie. His dad's voice softened. "I know, Mindy. I want to be with you, too. My plan was always to leave my wife, but then Melissa saw those kids murdered and they threw us into witness protection before I knew what was happening. We have to be patient. As soon as the trial is over and the men who want to harm my kids are in jail, I'll come back to you."

Joey gagged on cookie crumbs as he shot to his feet and ran down the hallway to his room. He sat on the edge of his bed, breathing hard, trying to make sense of his dad's conversation with someone named Mindy. Waking Jack wouldn't do any good. He was mad all the time, ever since they moved to Montana. Kendall would listen to him, though.

He snuck back out into the hall and approached his big sister's room. Rotating the knob as quietly as he could, he slipped into her room and closed the door behind him. Kendall kept her curtains shut, and it was pitch black in her bedroom. Joey waited for his eyes to see better in the dark. On his way to her bed, he tripped on something soft and bumped into the side of her mattress.

Kendall made a groaning sound, and Joey reached for her arm. "Kendall?" he whispered. "Ken? Are you awake?"

Another complaining noise came out of her throat. "Ash? Uh - crap. I mean, Joey? What's wrong?"

Hearing her voice made tears burn in his eyes. He wanted to cry but fought it. "Can I get in your bed?"

"Can't you sleep?"

"Kind of."

Kendall flipped her blankets back for him, and he climbed up onto her bed. He stuck his toes into the warmth, and his sister flung the covers over his shivering body. "What do you mean by kind of? You smell like chocolate and peanut butter. Did you sneak cookies?"

She tickled his sides, and his shoulders relaxed. "Maybe." He giggled quietly.

"And then you couldn't get back to sleep?"

He shook his head no. "I heard Dad talking to someone in the living room."

"Who?" Her voice sounded sleepy.

"I don't know. He was on the phone with somebody named Mindy." Beside him, Kendall's body stiffened.

"Are you sure? He's not supposed to talk to anyone from back home." Kendall sat up, pulling the covers with her. "What was he saying to her?"

Joey shrugged. "Something about floating banks and selling shells."

"What?"

"And..." Joey drew his knees up to his chest. He didn't want to say the next part.

"And what?"

"Never mind."

"Joey, what are you talking about? It sounds like you were sleepwalking."

He pushed himself up and shook his head hard. "I wasn't! I ate cookies! Besides... Dad said he planned to leave his wife after the trial. That's Mom, right?"

Kendall grabbed his shoulders. "You heard him say that, Joey? Are you sure?"

His sister sounded angry, and her fingers hurt as they dug into his skin. "What does he mean, Ken? Is Dad leaving?" His voice sounded like a baby, and he wiped his wet cheek with the back of his hand.

She pulled him into her chest and wrapped her arms tight around him. "I don't know. Everything is all messed up. I wish I had never seen what I saw."

"Did you really see kids get killed? I thought you just saw the bad guys."

Kendall kissed the top of his head. "I saw both, buddy. And now everything is screwed up. Listen," she drew back and looked into his eyes. She wiped his tears away with her thumbs. "Don't say anything about this to anyone until I find out what's going on. Okay? You don't want to get into trouble for sneaking cookies in the middle of the night, right?"

Joey shook his head. He didn't understand what was going on, but he was smart enough to know this trouble was way bigger than his midnight cookie run.

14

———

Kendall woke to Joey's bare foot pressing against the crook of her neck. "Ugh! Joey!" Little boy feet were the most disgusting things on earth! She shoved his legs away and sat up. Her alarm clock added to the insult by blaring that it was time to get going. "Go back to your room, now Joey. I have to get ready for school, and so do you."

Her little brother had purple smudges under his eyes from lack of sleep. It was no wonder. His life was already a huge disaster. Theirs all were, and everything was about to blow up even worse. And it was all her fault. She'd heard her parents argue about Mindy before. The woman was her dad's administrative assistant, and her mom didn't like her. Kendall shuddered. God! How cliché! Her dad was such an asshole!

"Are you going to talk to Dad about what I told you?" Joey's voice sounded small and afraid.

"I'll take care of it, buddy. Don't you worry. Now, go," she pushed him off the bed, "get dressed for school."

In the midst of her anger, she grew indignant. If her dad could call Mindy, why couldn't she talk to Fletcher? She grabbed her cellphone from the nightstand and scrolled through her Facebook feed. She went to Fletcher's page and saw a picture of him in a shirt and tie with his arm draped around Delaney Finch at the homecoming dance. How could he? Didn't he miss her the way she missed him? Kendall tossed her phone on her bed, buried her face in her pillow, and screamed.

"What's the matter with you?" Jack peered around her door frame.

"Nothing! Shut my door!"

Jack shrugged and slammed it.

Their mom yelled from the kitchen. "No door slamming! Hurry up, kids! Why is everyone so slow this morning?"

Kendall's heart sank to her belly. If only her mom knew what was going on behind her back. But she naively went about the house in a baggy sweatshirt and leggings with no makeup on, not realizing she was in a competition for her husband.

Kendall's dad yelled, "Come on, kids! If you hurry, I can drop you off on my way into town today. But I can't be late. I have an interview at nine o'clock."

Kendall didn't know if she could sit in the same car with her dad at the moment. She wouldn't be able to talk to him or even look at him, for that matter. What was it with guys? First, her dad, and now Fletcher? They were all cheating jerks! She took a deep breath and sent her gaze skyward to keep her sudden tears from running through her freshly applied mascara. "Coming!"

Normally, the three siblings fought for the shotgun seat, but that morning, Kendall didn't go for it. She sat next to Joey in the back, which resulted in Jack narrowing his eyes at her suspiciously.

They first dropped Joey off at the front of the elementary school. A cute little kid with black hair waved at him, and Kendall was glad her brother was making friends. On the drive to the high school, Jack asked if he could hang out with some of his new friends after school to shoot hoops in the gym.

"I suppose that's okay, but Jack, be careful as you start making friends. You must keep our family history a secret, and the more you share with the guys, the harder that will be."

"I know, Dad. I'm not an idiot. It's not like I can forget. Jeeze!" He got out of the car and slammed the door without saying goodbye.

Kendall slid across the rear seat and opened the door closest to the curb. She climbed out and then leaned back in. Looking her dad in the eye, she said, "You may want to follow your own advice, Dad. Pretty sure talking to Mindy is breaking all the rules."

His jaw dropped, and he pushed his glasses up his nose, but Kendall didn't wait to hear his response. He would only tell her lies.

Kendall followed Jack toward the doors at a much slower pace. His anger propelled him, in the same way her sorrow and loneliness held her back. She longed to have a friend with whom she could talk things through. Running her thumb over her phone screen, she yearned for Fletcher. She wanted him to hold her and tell her everything would be okay. But he was holding someone else now.

She supposed she couldn't blame him. But if he knew why she left so suddenly, he might feel differently. If he knew she still loved him, he never would have asked Delaney out. And if her dad could call his whore, why couldn't she contact Fletcher?

Kendall chewed her bottom lip all the way to her first-hour English Lit class until the skin was raw and flaking. She sat in the back row of the classroom but didn't take out her iPad because she'd had her mind fixed on Fletcher. She only had three more years until she turned eighteen. After that, Deputy Sterling told her she could do what she wanted.

She liked the federal deputies who watched over them. They said the Miller kids could call them by their first names, but that still felt a little weird. She practiced thinking of them that way. *Hank* was super cute, but he was like twice her age and besides, he preferred hanging out with her brothers. *Dirk* was super good-looking too, in a dark and almost dangerous sort of way. Mysterious. Kendall liked him the best because he seemed to get her. He cared that her heart was broken, and he sat with her while she cried about her parents fighting all the time. Dirk understood her fears. He made her feel safe. She wondered if he had kids of his own. He told her if she identified the killers, they'd go to prison for life, and she wouldn't have to worry about them anymore. She decided to direct-message Fletcher as soon as she got home from school and ask him to wait for her.

"Kendall? What do you think Shakespeare meant

when he wrote Orsino's first lines in Twelfth Night beginning with, 'If music be the food of love, play on.'?" Mrs. Blankenship, her English teacher, glowered at her from behind the lectern at the front of the room, tapping her pen on its edge. Startled out of her thoughts, Kendall sat up and fumbled to get her iPad out of her backpack. "Glad you decided to join us. We'll come back to you."

Several kids snickered at her, and their teacher moved on to another unsuspecting student. "Ryan? What are your thoughts?"

Mrs. Blankenship didn't rattle the kid named Ryan, even though he didn't have his iPad out either. He stretched his cowboy-booted feet out before him and looped his arm around the back of his chair. He sent their teacher a sly grin. "I'm pretty sure the duke just wanted to get into Olivia's pants, and since that wasn't happening, he wanted to get over his feelings for her."

His friends laughed at his audacity, which both shocked and intrigued Kendall. She couldn't believe the boy would dare to say something so crass to their teacher. Ryan winked at her when he noticed her looking at him and Kendall's cheeks flushed with heat.

Unbelievably, Mrs. Blankenship nodded her head. "I don't appreciate your word choice, Ryan, but yes, in a sense, I agree. And thank you for doing your reading assignment. That will make today's homework much easier for you. As for the majority of you who did not read the assignment, you will need to do that before you answer the Scene-One Review questions. You'll find them in Schoology, and they are due by 11:59 pm tonight."

Kendall *had* done the assignment posted in the school

software program, but thoughts of Fletcher distracted her. Maybe he was like Orsino—wanting to get over her. A dull ache thudded in her heart. She was dealing with so much crap. The teacher had no idea. It wasn't like she could share her struggles with anyone. She had no one but Fletcher, and he was supposedly off limits.

But surely, she could trust him to keep her new identity a secret... couldn't she?

15

Emory tapped her freshly manicured nails on her desk, trying to ease her nerves. She hadn't talked with Dirk since she walked out on their date. She half expected him to come after her when she left, but he didn't. And now she wasn't sure where they stood. It had been her idea to talk about their relationship in a public place so there wouldn't be any arguing or raised voices, but her plan backfired when she realized she was the one who got too emotional.

Now, her nerves zipped around inside her stomach like hot electrical wires. Her heart lurched when she heard the bell of the elevator car stopping on their floor, and she held her breath. But it was Teresa who entered the office.

"Morning, Chief." Teresa put her purse in the bottom drawer of her desk. "How's your coffee? Want a warmup?"

Emory forced her shoulders to relax and pressed them down. "Sure, thanks."

Teresa brought her a fresh cup, and after handing it to

her, leaned against the doorjamb of Emory's office. "Are you feeling okay?"

"Yes, why?"

Tilting her head to the side, Teresa considered Emory. "You look tired. Rough night?"

If she only knew. Emory nodded and patted her cheeks with enough slap to get some color in her face. "I didn't sleep well. I guess I need this coffee more than I realized." She laughed, but it sounded hollow, and Teresa narrowed her gaze speculatively. Emory changed the subject. "Are you and Tomas coming to Thanksgiving dinner at Dirk's house? Laurie Dillinger and her little boy, Caleb, will be there, so Tomas will have someone to play with."

"Yeah, thanks. It'll be nice to share the holiday with everyone. Thanks for organizing it."

"Of course. But honestly, it's a little self-serving. My parents can't grill me too horribly with a bunch of other people present." Emory grinned and drew in a life-giving sip of dark-roasted coffee.

"Grill you about what?" Teresa raised her brows. "Dirk?"

"Well, about my future. You know... when am I going to get married and give them grandkids, blah blah blah..." Emory forced her tone to sound flippant. "You know, I'm giving the entire office Friday off, so you won't need to use any PTO to stay home with Tomas. Does he have any other days off that week?"

"Yeah." Teresa's posture slumped. "He has the full week off for fall break." She sighed. "When did schools start having a fall break? We never got that as kids."

"I don't know, but I don't want you to worry about it, Teresa. Maybe you can work remotely on those days?"

Teresa brightened. "Really? That would be great. You're the best, Chief. Thanks!"

Henry's laugh sounded from down the hallway. Emory hadn't heard the guys arrive, and with Dirk's sudden appearance, her hand trembled. She spilled coffee on her slacks.

"Morning, Teresa. Chief." Henry flashed them his boyish smile.

Dirk followed his junior partner into the office. He did not smile, and his dark gaze clashed with hers. He didn't look away and his intensity caused heat to rush up her neck and fill her cheeks. Emory pushed her chair back and rose to her feet. "The briefing is early today. Be in the conference room by eight-thirty." She raised her chin and walked with mock confidence out of the office and down the hall to the restroom, where she soaked several paper towels with cool water and held them against her face before attending to the stain on her pants.

She should never have gotten involved with a man in her office. She knew better. After mentally chastising herself, she sighed. Who was she kidding? What she and Dirk had was no mere fling, and he deserved better than for her to just walk out on their conversation. But he'd been hinting at breaking up, and she didn't want there to be a scene. Now, here she was, doing exactly the same thing again. At the office, no less.

Emory glared at her reflection in the mirror. "Get ahold of yourself," she murmured aloud.

By the time she returned to the office, her team was waiting for her around the conference table. She strode in with as much confidence as she could fake and took her place at the head of the room. "Anything to report on the Miller family?"

Henry glanced at Dirk and then answered, "Nothing since yesterday."

"Good." Emory pressed on. "Teresa, I know you don't want to cross the lines between work and home, but has Tomas mentioned anything more about Joey?"

"No, not really. He told me that the new kid was hanging with a threesome of troublemakers. But they're eight. How much trouble can they get in?"

Emory glanced at her notes. "Okay, thanks. Dirk and Henry, have either of you come up with leads on any of the top hundred most wanted list?"

Dirk answered, and she forced herself to look at him, doing her best to do so with no emotion showing on her face. "Yeah. One of my informants coughed up some info on a dirtbag named Doug Bergman. He's wanted for violating the conditions of a supervised release and for firing on law enforcement officers. My guy claims he heard Bergman is in town to see his ex-girlfriend, so we'll head out this morning and see what we can find."

"Okay, sounds good." Emory dropped her gaze and kept her head down as if she were reading something from her iPad. "You two will probably be out of the office for the rest of the day, so on a personal note, Dirk, what time do you want everyone to show up at your house for Thanksgiving?"

He didn't answer until all eyes in the room, including

Emory's, were on him. Finally, once she met his gaze, he shrugged. "I wasn't sure we were still having dinner together... but if we are, two o'clock should be good. How many should I plan for, again?"

Emory's pulse rattled like a drum roll in her chest, but she took a steadying breath and said, "As far as I know, the number hasn't changed. I'm looking forward to celebrating with all of you." She gathered her things and stood. "Be careful out there today, guys." Emory tossed a vague glance in Henry and Dirk's direction and then focused on her admin. "Teresa, I need you to help me with a few projects in my office."

Henry and Teresa shared a wide-eyed glance with each other, communicating a silent message that Emory interpreted as they knew something awkward was going on between her and Dirk. Without acknowledging their curiosity, she marched out of the meeting, went directly to her office, and closed the door.

Moments later, a knock sounded. Emory cleared her throat. "Come in."

Teresa slid into the room and shut the door behind her. "Is everything alright? You seemed kind of off in the meeting. If you aren't feeling well, I can handle the office today. Especially if Sterling and Flannigan are going to be out."

"No." Emory released a huge pent-up breath. "I'll be fine. I'm just tired. I may cut out early, but I have plenty of work I have to get done this morning." She would use that excuse to stay locked inside her office until the guys left. She and Dirk needed to hash things out and determine how it all would play out at work. But that conversation had to happen another time and somewhere other than the office.

"Remember when you said you wanted us to be friends?" Teresa crossed her arms over her chest.

Emory peered up at her. "Yes."

"Well, as your friend, I'm telling you that you and Sterling should take a few minutes and grab a cup of coffee or something before they head out. He shouldn't be distracted when he's on a mission and you... well... you won't get any work done until you fix whatever is going on."

A defensive wave of emotion rose in Emory's throat, and she wondered why she had ever let herself become personally involved with her staff. She knew better, and now here she was in the middle of an office drama. Her father would remind her there was a reason officers didn't socialize with the enlisted ranks in the military.

"I'll handle it. Thank you, Teresa. I'll call you when I'm ready for your administrative help. Please close the door on your way out."

16

———

D irk drove with Hank riding shotgun, and as he suspected, it wasn't long before his partner could no longer resist satisfying his curiosity. "What's going on between you and the chief?"

"Nothing." He didn't want to hash the whole mess out with Hank.

"Yeah, right. What'd you do to piss her off?"

"Nothing." *Just crushed her hopes and dreams.*

"If you don't want to talk about it, just say so."

"Okay, I don't want to talk about it."

"Well, whatever is going on is affecting the whole team. You both act like T and I can't see the looks passing between the two of you, but the tension in the office is thicker than pea soup. Are we still on for Thanksgiving or what?"

"She said we were."

"Yeah, but if you two are fighting, it's going to be really uncomfortable for the rest of us."

"We're not fighting, Hank. Emory said we are having

Thanksgiving at my place, so that's what's we're doing." Before Hank could pry any farther into his business, Dirk turned the tables on him. "How are things going between you and Amy? Any progress?"

Hank's shoulders drooped as he released a deep sigh. "No. It's not good. The marriage counseling isn't helping. In fact, getting together once a week to see the therapist just gives Amy a consistent opportunity to complain about my failings as a husband."

"Therapy only works if people truly want to get better."

"Yeah. I think she's just going so she can check off the box and justify asking me for a divorce."

Dirk glanced at Hank's defeated countenance. "I'm sorry, man. Is she coming for Thanksgiving?"

"I never asked her. Honestly, I don't want to ruin everyone's holiday with our personal drama. I think I'll come solo."

"Probably best."

"You geared up to have 'the talk' with the chief's father?"

"We'll see. I think we should all just focus on the food and leave the rest alone. Holidays are never a good time for serious discussions." Dirk's gut squirmed. The last thing in the world he wanted was to face Emory's two-star Marine Corps General father and confess that he'd broken the man's favorite daughter's heart.

Dirk could see that Hank wanted to ask him more about it, but finally he shrugged. "As long as you know I'm here for you if you need me."

"Appreciate that."

They pulled to the side of a gravel road on the outskirts of Billings that led to a row of old, abandoned grain elevators. It was a lonely place that addicts and other transient people had taken over and made home. Homeless folks had pitched more tents around the outside of the towering cylinders than Dirk had seen before. The habitants had bundled up with whatever they had to ward off the cold. Some lay across tent openings, others sat propped against the crumbling concrete silos. Most of them were either sleeping or were strung out on a drug-induced mental vacation.

Dirk slid the opening of his jacket behind his holster, allowing the silver US Marshal's badge he wore clipped to his belt to show. "Anyone here know Zig Zag?" He called out. His confidential informant had named himself after a brand of cigarette rolling paper. Pairs of glassy eyes from the vagrant population regarded Dirk and Hank. Most offered them blank stares. A few others vaguely wagged their heads.

One man, wearing only a thin cotton shirt and sweatpants with holes in the knees, waved his hand toward a dirt path leading to a small, abandoned building behind the elevators. Dirk guessed the rickety shed had once served as an office. "ZZ gets his Zs over there." The man laughed at his own joke, causing himself to erupt in a coughing fit which worked itself into a wet, phlegmy hack.

"Thanks." Dirk stepped off toward the building, and Hank followed.

"Don't you have this guy's phone number? How does

he contact you?" Hank's words puffed white in the cold air, and he pulled the lapels of his coat together.

"He had one, but I can't reach him on it." Dirk flipped the collar of his leather jacket up to keep the frigid breeze from blowing down his neck. "He probably sold it for a fix."

"Is this guy reliable?"

Dirk raised a brow and tilted his head to look at Hank. "As reliable as any drug-addicted confidential informant." He chuckled. "As far as informants go, Zig Zag is pretty good when he's somewhat sober."

"Did he call you with the phone you gave him?"

"Yep."

"What did he tell you?"

They approached the shack. The opening which used to hold a door on brass hinges was now a gaping hole that emitted a dank, dirty-body smell. Dirk peered inside at eight to ten people draped in various positions around the room. All of them were stoned out of their minds. "Zig Zag, you in here?" He waited for a response. "Ziggy?"

Someone in the pile groaned and rolled over, causing two others to complain. "Sterling?" A scrawny man pushed himself up to a sitting position. "That you?"

"Yeah, Zig, it's me. You never called me back."

Confusion settled on the man's drooping features. "Call you back?"

"Come out of there, so we can talk." Dirk waited for Zig Zag to untangle himself from the heap of broken humanity and climb to his feet. Once they were outside, Dirk continued. "You left a message for me about seeing Chance Bergman. You said you could help me find him."

"Oh... that's right. And your message said you'd buy me dinner." Zig Zag narrowed his rheumy eyes under graying hair he hadn't washed or even combed in a long time. "When are you gonna make good on that promise?"

"I would have done it sooner if you had returned my call, Zig. It took me a while to hunt you down. I'm going to have to take the phone back if you won't return my calls, you know."

Zig Zag scratched at a rash of scabs on his cheek. "No, man. Don't do that. I'll do better. You'll see."

"Okay, well, get your stuff and let's go to lunch. We need to talk, and I'd rather not do it here. Besides, I can see your bones right through your clothes. You look like you could stand a warm meal."

Dirk's CI wobbled as he got to his feet, dragging a filthy swath of cloth behind him. "Let's go."

Dirk led the way to his Jeep and opened the door for Ziggy. As Hank and the informant got settled in the vehicle, Dirk popped the back hatch and pulled out a wool blanket he kept in there along with some power bars and water in case of an emergency, like getting stuck in a blizzard. He walked back to the man who had directed him to Zig Zag.

"Hey, buddy, thanks for your help." He handed his blanket and other items to the sparsely dressed man. "Try to stay warm out here, okay?"

The man blinked up at Dirk and smiled, displaying the rotted teeth of a meth user. "Thanks, man."

Dirk nodded and jogged back to his Jeep. As soon as the engine roared, he cranked the heat. "It's F-ing cold out there. Ziggy, I don't understand why you don't get sober and put a roof over your head."

"Yeah, yeah. A guy like you won't ever get it, Sterling. I just take life as it comes, and right now, I want that hot dinner you're gonna buy me."

"Right. No problem. *After* you give me the information I'm looking for."

"Who's this pretty boy you're driving around? He another snitch?"

"Nah, this is my partner, Hank."

Ziggy continued, as though Hank couldn't hear him. "You trust him? Cuz, I don't know him."

"With my life."

"Hm." Ziggy eyed Hank, who raised his chin at him in greeting.

"Good to meet you," Hank said. "I asked Sterling the same thing about you. I guess if he trusts you, I should."

Ziggy crossed his skinny arms over his chest. "My jury's still out on you, boy. I'll keep you posted. If I've learned one thing, it's that there's not a lot of folks worth trusting."

17

H ank held the door for Zig Zag as he spilled out of the back of Dirk's Rubicon. The CI lost his balance when he stood, and Hank caught him before he fell to the pavement.

"Thanks, man." Zig Zag climbed hand over hand up Hank's coat sleeve until he regained his stability.

Dirk's eyes sparked with humor, but his features remained hard. He was in his bad-ass interview mode. "Quit screwing around, Z. Let's get this over with." Dirk held the door for them, and they entered the small diner.

It was one of those places with a 1950s theme where the waitresses all wore bombshell-red lipstick and called you 'Hon'. For the day's lunch rush of three tables, only one woman manned the dining room in front of the single-cook galley. The other occupied tables held folks who'd stopped in for a burger, or to get out of the cold with a hot cup of Joe, or both. Something cooking in the kitchen smelled tasty, and Hank's stomach rumbled in anticipation.

Hank studied the space. He figured there was a back door through the kitchen. He casually noted the exit on the side of the dining room by the restrooms. The two men who sat together at a booth both looked like they could handle themselves if they needed to, and the older couple would stay out of the way if anything out of the ordinary happened. Hank saw Dirk making a similar mental sweep of the room. Basic law enforcement behavior. They chose a table in the back corner where both Hank and Dirk took seats facing the dining room.

The gum-smacking server, a woman in her fifties with brown hair teased and pinned up in a topknot, and wearing thick-soled tennis shoes, approached their table. "You boys here for lunch or just coffee?"

"Lunch, please." Dirk accepted a menu from her, and she passed two more to Hank and Z.

"Today's special is pot-roast and mashed potatoes. And I got a fresh baked apple pie if you're still hungry. I'll bring water. Anything else to drink?"

Hank and Dirk declined, but Z wrapped his hands around the thick empty cup on the table before him. "Fill this mug up with hot coffee and keep it coming. It's colder than a witch's tit out there."

The server glowered at him and turned on her heel. Dirk slid out of his jacket and hung it on the back of his chair. "Z don't talk like that in front of a lady. If you can't behave, we'll have to have this conversation outside."

"Yeah, yeah."

The waitress returned right away with Ziggy's coffee. "This ought to warm you up." She filled his cup and set the carafe next to him. "Have you all decided what you're hungry for?"

They made it easy for her and each ordered the special. After they savored the first few bites of beef with brown gravy, Dirk eyed Z. "So, what do you have to tell me?"

Zig Zag took forever to chew and swallow the food in his mouth. "Well, you see, I heard some guys talking about this other dude they called Chance. Said he was coming back to town, and they's all acting scared and shit."

"And..." Dirk filled the empty mug next to his plate from the carafe.

"Hey! That's my coffee, Sterling!" Ziggy reached across the table for the pitcher.

Hank grabbed his arm just above the elbow and at his wrist. He slid into the chair next to Zig Zag and twisted his arm behind his back and wrenched it upward. "Pretty sure Deputy Marshal Sterling here told you to mind your manners. Finish answering his question."

Ziggy squirmed but couldn't get free. "Let go of me, and I will."

"Answer and I'll let go." Hank pressed Ziggy's elbow an inch higher up his spine.

"Okay, okay!" Hank eased the pressure on the informant's arm, but kept hold of it. "So, I listened in to see if I heard anything that might be useful to you."

Dirk scoffed. "Yeah right. Cut the crap. You listened to see if there was a way to use the information to get something you wanted, either drugs from your cronies or food from me. Go on."

Z let out a sigh. "Okay, so anyway, they were whispering about some bad dude named Chance something-or-other who was coming back to town, even though it was dangerous to show his face around here."

"Why is it dangerous?" Hank asked.

"I don't know. Stop interrupting me." Ziggy glared at Hank, who continued to hold him in place and away from his food. "Maybe cuz he knows the cops are looking for him. Anyway, he's going to be at his girlfriend's house tomorrow around supper time. That's all I know. Now let me go!" He jerked his shoulders, and Hank released him. As fast as he could, Z scooped a huge spoonful of meat and gravy into his mouth.

Dirk leaned forward. "What else do you know, Zig? What *aren't* you telling us?"

"Nothing, man. I swear!" Ziggy crammed in another mouthful of potatoes.

"Who were the guys who were talking about Bergman? Did they know you were listening to them?"

"Don't know. Not the regular guys. I think they were just buying—you know? They were talking to each other. I pretended to be passed out, so they don't know I heard. But when they said Bergman, I remembered the name from a while back when a guy by that name killed a cop. I figured you'd want to know."

Dirk eased back in his chair. "You figured right. If this is the man we've been looking for and we arrest him, the US Marshals Office is offering a reward."

Hank stared Z down. "What would you do with the reward money, Ziggy? It could mean a new lease on life. You could get help to get clean and start over."

Ziggy eyed Hank with suspicion. "Yeah. That's what I'd do, for sure."

Hank chuffed. If the marshals rewarded this tweaker with the money, he'd probably end up dead from all the smack he'd buy. What a waste. "Sounds like a good plan, then. It's best if you tell us every detail you can remember. Who is Bergman's girlfriend? Where does she live?"

"How the hell would I know? They didn't give me her business card."

"That's, too bad." Hank frowned and shook his head. "I feel the reward money slipping away. No info, no cash. That's how it works, Ziggy."

The waitress removed their plates and returned to take their dessert order. Dirk held up two fingers. "Just two slices of that pie, please. I'll have mine with ice-cream. How about you, Hank?"

"Oh, yeah. Gotta have ice cream. Thanks!"

"Come on, guys!" Ziggy complained. "I want pie, too! I told you some good stuff!"

"Yeah, but not enough for dessert." Dirk refilled his coffee and took a sip.

"I don't know nothing else!"

"Thing is, Ziggy, I don't believe that. Do you, Hank?"

Hank shook his head sadly. "Nope. And it's too bad, too, because that pie looks delicious."

"Okay, okay. I heard them say something about the chick's house being over the backside of Old Mill Hill. I don't know which one it is, but there's a bunch of trailers over there."

Dirk nodded. "That's about all there is over there. You're sure they said tomorrow?"

"Yeah. I'm sure."

"Okay, I want you to look at some pictures. You tell me if any of them are the men you heard talking about Bergman." Dirk turned his phone so Ziggy could see the screen and slowly scrolled through a set of twenty pictures.

Ziggy tapped the screen when Dirk flipped to a photo of a known associate of Bergman's named Mack Rogers. "This guy. Yep. He was one of them."

"You're sure?"

"Yeah. Scary looking dude. I wouldn't forget him."

Dirk bobbed his head at Hank, who raised his hand for the waitress. "We'll have a third slice of pie."

"Coming right up." The woman grinned, and Hank wondered if Dirk regularly brought informants to this diner. He leaned into Ziggy's slight shoulder. "This information better pan out, Zig Zag. Because if it doesn't, I'll put the word out that you're a snitch and you won't last through the afternoon."

Ziggy's eyes flew open. "You wouldn't do that! Sterling! You said I could trust this dude."

"You can, so long as the info you gave us proves to be useful."

18

Teresa balanced two bags of groceries in one arm as she unlocked the front door. "Tomas, what homework do you have tonight?"

"Spelling, math, and I have to write a paragraph about Sitting Bull."

"Oh, I almost forgot. When is your field trip to the Western Heritage Center?"

Tomas tossed his backpack on the couch. "Friday. Ms. Fields said I still need to turn in my permission slip. What's for snack?"

Teresa set the groceries on the counter of her tiny kitchen and rummaged through one of the bags. She pulled out a package of off-brand Oreos. "How about cookies and milk?" It wasn't the healthiest choice. In fact, she'd seen a social post the other day that showed someone unsuccessfully trying to melt a similar sandwich cookie with a blowtorch. Giving her son such undigestible treats proved she was lacking in the "good mom" department. Images of herself baking homemade goodies while wearing an apron and a smile made her chest feel tight. She closed her eyes, cleared her throat, and pushed the damning thoughts away. Some days... strike that... most days she whittled her version of motherhood down to survival, which meant providing Tomas with whatever was the cheapest and easiest.

"Yes!" Her son ran to the refrigerator and got out the milk while she placed four cookies on a plate for him.

"Sit at the table to do your homework and eat." Tomas yanked a worn spiral notebook from his pack and practiced writing out his spelling words between dipping cookies into his milk. Teresa put a kettle on the stove. The sky darkened with storm clouds, and she could think of nothing better at the moment than a hot cup of strong tea. "How did things go between you and the new boy today?" She surprised herself by asking Tomas about Joey Miller after getting irritated at Emory for suggesting she do it. But the kid hadn't treated Tomas very well, and her mama bear instincts had kicked in.

"Good." Her son chomped on a soggy chocolate cookie. "We played soccer together at lunch recess."

"What about Brett and the other boys?"

"They didn't want to play."

She wanted to know more but decided to avoid making an issue out of a forgotten playground spat. It sounded like Tomas dealt with the bullies well enough. In times like these, she tried to find a balance between over-mothering and giving him a strong, solid influence as well. It was impossible to be both mom and dad to her son. Maybe she could get Dirk to talk to him about it. He was great with kids, and it wouldn't be the first time she'd asked him to play a fatherly role that she was unable to fill.

Teresa quizzed Tomas on his words. He missed three out of ten and wrote the correct spelling for them five times each. After he blazed through his multiplication problems, he brushed his bangs out of his eyes and looked up at her. "Mom, can Joey come over here to play sometime?"

A large part of her wanted to say absolutely not. She didn't appreciate blurring the lines between work and home. Could Tomas possibly be in any danger if he hung out with the Miller boy? Probably not, and Tomas didn't have many friends. She hedged. "I don't know, bud. It's hard since you have after-school care."

The kettle whistled angrily, and she was thankful for the interruption. Tomas's warm dark eyes regarded her as she fixed her English Breakfast tea. "What about on a Saturday... like *this* Saturday?"

She breathed in the robust, slightly malty scent of her drink. "I'd have to meet his parents first, and I'm sure they'd want to meet us." There was another problem. They'd ask what she did for a living, and she'd have to admit she worked with the marshals.

"Joey said I was lucky to have just one parent. He said his mom and dad yell at each other all the time."

"Well, sometimes parents argue. That's normal." However, Teresa wondered if it was normal in the Millers' case or if the stress of changing their entire lives was getting to them.

"Will you call them and ask if Joey can come over? Please, Mom? *Please?*"

There were so many reasons to discourage this friendship, but her son's pleading eyes decided for her. "I'll think about it. Maybe after Thanksgiving." Teresa would ask Emory what she thought about encouraging the boys' friendship in the morning. She knew she'd have to draw some firm boundaries. The last thing she wanted was to become a narc on Tomas's friend.

EMORY UNLOCKED THE OFFICE DOOR, and after dumping her coat and bag on her desk, she went to start the day's first pot of coffee. On her way, she ran her fingertips along the back of Dirk's chair. She missed how things were between them before she'd brought up having kids. She wished she'd never said anything.

Emory hadn't slept well the previous night for worrying about Thanksgiving. It was her party, but Dirk had agreed to host the dinner at his house. She'd given her parents the impression there was a future between Dirk and her, and God only knew what her dad was going to say to him. Whatever it was, it wouldn't be good. Her father hadn't yet accepted that she was a grown woman, and he still viewed himself as her protector. She hoped Dirk could field his interrogation without letting it ruin the entire holiday.

Teresa called out when she entered the office. "Morning, Chief."

Emory poked her head out the door of the break room. "How did you know it was me?"

A bright laugh lit up Teresa's face. "Educated guess.

Sterling and Flannigan never get here before eight-thirty." She hung up her coat and dropped her purse in the bottom file drawer of her desk.

"True." Emory took her first sip of the rich, much-needed coffee.

"So, Boss, I have a question for you. I know that before, I said I was against mixing work with home life, but Tomas unknowingly has put me in that position. The WITSEC kid, Joey Miller, is in Tomas's class, and the boys are becoming friends."

"That's nice. I don't see any conflict with that."

"Except Tomas wants Joey to come to our house to play next weekend. That means I have to meet Joey's parents. What happens when I tell them where I work?"

"Ah, I see." She drew in another sip as she thought it over. "I realize this probably feels muddy. But knowing you're a deputy marshal should make them feel more secure. They'd be certain their son would be perfectly safe with you. And honestly, the whole family is safer if we have a view of the inside track."

Teresa frowned. "Maybe. Or else they might think we're keeping too close of tabs on them. For example, Joey told Tomas his parents fight all the time."

Emory shrugged. "What they think is up to them. And arguing is normal, especially when two people are under the kind of stress they're dealing with."

"I don't like using Tomas for my work."

"I agree, and I'm not asking you to. It's best to let the boys' friendship develop naturally. If it does, fine. If it doesn't, that's also fine."

"But you're okay with it?"

"Yes. Though I might have Dirk and Henry look in on them again, just in case. But you should treat the situation like you would if Joey was any other kid."

The guys were late for the morning meeting, and Emory and Teresa waited for them in the conference room.

When they arrived, Henry at least had the decency to look chagrined as he slid into his usual chair next to Teresa. "Sorry, Chief."

Dirk poured himself a cup of coffee and took his seat across from her, saying nothing.

"Nice of you guys to come to work today." Teresa teased.

Dirk addressed Teresa rather than Emory. "We were already at work while you were sleeping peacefully in your warm bed. Hank and I were out most of the night doing recon to find Chance Bergman's girlfriend's place. We received some intel yesterday that Bergman is planning a visit, so we checked out the trailer park where Ziggy had heard she lived."

Henry opened his laptop, clicked a few keys, and turned it so the women could view his screen. "She lives in this trailer park neighborhood, which is on the other side of Old Mill Hill where we set up surveillance last night to monitor the place."

Dirk pointed to the screen. "We believe we found Bergman's girlfriend. The woman in question arrived at the trailer park north of town yesterday evening in a beat-up Toyota Corolla. She was followed by a man in an Army-green F150. The truck is registered to Mack Rogers —the man Ziggy identified as the guy he heard talking about Bergman at the grain elevators. We recognized him when he got out of his vehicle and spoke with the woman. After several minutes of conversation, Rogers climbed back in his vehicle and drove away. The woman went inside her home."

Emory quietly stared at Dirk until he grudgingly swung his gaze toward her and raised his brows to acknowledge her. She asked, "When do you think Bergman will show?"

Dirk held her gaze. "Tonight. If my CI is correct."

"Good. Both of you, take the afternoon off and get some sleep. Sounds like you'll be up late again tonight. But on your way home, I want you to stop by the Millers' house. Rumor has it that James and Ann are fighting regularly."

Dirk's black brows dipped together. "Where did you hear that?"

Teresa leaned her head back and sighed. "Apparently, Tomas has befriended Joey." She caught the guys up on her talk with her son.

"Sounds about right." Dirk rubbed the dark whiskers shadowing his chin. "Last couple of times we stopped by, they were fighting. I don't think they've called the therapist yet, either."

Emory rolled her lower lip inward and bit down. "I wonder if the protection program is going to end up splitting their family entirely."

19

Heat radiated from Kendall's neck and face. Even her ears were hot as she carried her lunch tray across the school cafeteria to an empty table. It seemed every pair of eyes in the room followed her. There was nothing worse than sitting alone at lunch. She pictured a sign flashing *LOSER* over her head that everyone could see. She couldn't wait until she got her driver's license and could go somewhere off-campus to eat.

Kendall glimpsed her brother looking for a place to sit. He'd made friends already. It was easy for him because of sports. She'd been a cheerleader before, but now she was a nobody. She raised her hand and waved. "Easton!" As soon as she said his real name, the fiery blood that had been pulsing in her cheeks drained from her face, and she stuffed her hand in her lap.

Jack glanced around to see if anyone noticed. He approached Kendall's table and slid his tray next to hers. "Smooth."

"Sorry. It's hard to change how I think of you."

"I know. No big deal. No one was paying any attention." He folded his legs over the bench seat and stretched them out under the table. "If we get busted, we could pretend it's just my nickname..." His voice dropped low and matched the dim light in his eyes. "But that would only work if I was allowed to play baseball. The Easton brand isn't exactly known for their football or basketball equipment."

"I feel so bad about you having to give up your baseball dreams, E." Kendall rolled her eyes. "I mean, Jack. This whole thing really sucks. I know." She took a bite of her tasteless salad and added more ranch dressing while she studied her brother. Deciding she could trust him, she ventured sharing her secret. "Don't tell anyone, but I've been stalking my old friends on Insta and Facebook."

"Kendall, you can't do that! It's dangerous." Jack glared at her and pushed his tray away. "If the mob finds us, all our sacrifices will be for nothing."

"No one can see me lurking on the site. I created a fake profile. Besides, I'm not commenting or even liking anything. I'm just looking." Her chest compressed, and a sad sigh escaped. "Fletcher took Delaney Finch to the homecoming dance. He's such a jerk!"

Jack rested his hand on her shoulder. "He's not being a jerk, Ken. It's not like he's cheating on you. You're not there anymore. I know it blows, but you need to move on, too."

Kendall felt like she'd swallowed a stone. "I don't know why *I* have to, when Dad doesn't." The words flew out of her mouth before she'd thought about them. Now it was too late.

"What do you mean?"

Kendall groaned. "I guess you should know, too. Last night, Joey snuck into the kitchen for some cookies and overheard Dad talking to Mindy."

"Who's Mindy?"

"His old admin from his office in New York. But it's even worse than that. Joey came to my room and asked if he could sleep in my bed. He said he heard Dad say he was leaving Mom to be with Mindy."

Flame ignited in Jack's eyes as he stared at her and grappled with what she had told him. Finally, he growled, "That son of a bitch!"

"Right? I guess it sort of doesn't surprise me. I mean, Mom and Dad fight all the time."

"So, he puts all of us in danger for a piece of ass?"

"I don't know. The whole thing makes me sick. I feel so bad for Mom."

"We could tell on him, you know, to the marshals."

Kendall's shoulders dropped. "What good would that do? It won't fix their marriage. I heard Deputy Sterling tell them they should go to a therapist, but I doubt they will."

"I guess Mom really will have to get a job. That'll be weird. What's going to happen, do you think? If they get divorced, will the marshals move Dad to another secret place?"

"I don't know." Kendall dropped her fork onto her tray. "I wish none of this ever happened."

"Yeah, well, it sounds like Dad was gonna leave us,

anyway. That has nothing to do with us being... you know... in hiding. Does Mom know?"

"I'm not sure. I'm only going on what Joey heard, and he's only eight. Maybe he got the entire conversation screwed up." A miniscule flicker of hope lightened her misery.

"Even *he's* not that dumb."

Kendall shook her head, disgusted with the whole situation. Her wish extinguished. "He was pretty upset."

"Yeah, poor kid."

IT THRILLED Joey that they were learning how to play basketball in gym class. Maybe he'd get good enough to keep up with Jack. His brother hated playing with him now, because Joey never made a basket, and he always had to chase the ball. During the first part of class, each kid got a ball, and they all practiced dribbling. Then they had to make two lines and work on passing the ball to the kid opposite them. Tomas lined up across from Joey. It was tons more fun to play with a kid his own size. Deputy Hank always let him win, and that was boring.

At the far end of the gymnasium, they learned to shoot on baskets that were a lot shorter than the ones at the park by his house, and Joey made it in a bunch of times. Tomas was pretty good, too. Joey bounce-passed the ball to him. "We should check out a ball during lunch recess so we can play some more."

Tomas grinned. "Yeah!"

It was pizza day in the cafeteria, which was awesome,

and Joey sat next to Tomas. They gobbled up their pepperoni and cheesy pie as fast as they could and downed their milk, so they'd be the first in line to go outside. Tomas signed for their basketball, and as soon as the lunch bell rang and the recess monitor opened the door, they bolted to the court.

The baskets on the school playground were lower than the ones at Joey's home park, too. Maybe Jack would come here to play with him one day. Joey dreamed of impressing his big brother with what he had learned.

Joey lined up for a shot. He bent his knees like the gym teacher showed and held the ball up, but Brett ran up to him and slapped it out of his hands before he could shoot. The basketball bounced away, and one of Brett's gang snatched it up.

"Why are you playing with Tomas, Joey? I told you he's a dweeb." Brett sneered at Tomas, who ignored the bully and settled his dark eyes on Joey instead.

Joey shook off the urge to shove Brett and shrugged. He perched his hands on his hips. "Come on, Brett. Give us back our ball and leave us alone."

Brett pushed Joey back a step. "If you want it, you have to play with us. But Mendez is out."

Joey's stomach fisted into a hard knot. "Come on, guys. Just give us the ball."

Brett shoved harder, and Joey fell backward on to the blacktop, skinning his palms and elbows on the rough surface. "Get up, you big sissy. I'm starting to get why you want to hang out with Tomas. Cuz you're both babies."

Joey got to his feet, only to be tripped from behind by another of Brett's crew.

"Knock it off, you guys." Tomas lunged toward Brett, his fists curled at his sides.

The bully bumped his chest against Tomas's. "Yeah, Mendez? And what are you gonna do if we don't?" Brett thrust his hands against Tomas's shoulders, but Tomas chop blocked him and shoved back.

Surprised and embarrassed, Brett swung, hitting Tomas in the face. Joey jumped to his feet and ran at Brett, wrapping his arms around the bigger boy's middle and tackling him the way Jack taught him to when they played football. Brett landed on the rough surface and tore the elbow of his coat. He threw an arm around Joey and rolled on top of him, drawing his fist back.

Whistles sounded, but not in time to stop the blow. Brett struck Joey's nose and sparklers lit behind his eyes. Warm blood flowed from his nostrils over his mouth.

"Boys! Stop it right this minute!" The recess monitor ran to them and yanked Brett off Joey's stomach. "What is going on here? Brett Andrews, what do you think you're doing?"

"He hit me first!" Brett cried.

"No!" Joey climbed to his feet, wiping blood from his nose on his arm. "Brett hit Tomas first."

The recess monitor looked at Tomas, whose eye socket was red and turning purple. "That's it. All three of you are going to the principal's office. Let's go!" She grasped a handful of Brett's shirt as she marched them inside the school. Clearly, she knew who the real trouble-maker was. "Joey and Tomas, you two go to the nurse's office first, and when she's through with you, join us with Principal Thompson."

The nurse pressed a cold pack on Tomas's eye and cleaned up Joey's skinned places and his nose. The boys grinned at each other across the room, proud of their injuries. One thing was certain, Brett and his friends were now Joey's enemies. He'd made a decision he couldn't undo, but that was fine with him. Tomas was way more fun anyhow. The only bad part was Joey's parents would for sure ground him for fighting, so getting to hang out with Tomas after school was going to have to wait.

20

———

Volodymyr sat in a buttery leather chair in the opulent library of his estate in Deal, New Jersey. He puffed on his favorite silver pipe as he stared into the fire that crackled and blazed on the hearth. Deep in thought, he tapped the sterling mouthpiece gently against his teeth. It had been weeks, and still no one had any idea where the Bennington family had disappeared to. The trial date was looming, and he needed the threat of Melissa Bennington eradicated.

His father had asked for his help on an extremely lucrative drug deal, but until he was out of the police spotlight, he was hesitant to commit. The last thing he wanted to do was bring more attention from law enforcement to the family.

Mishka entered the room and stood to his side with his hands folded in front of him, waiting patiently to be acknowledged. Volodymyr waved his pipe at him, indicating that he should state the reason for his visit.

"Sir, have you decided whether to shake hands on

the deal with Tato Hordiyenko?" Mishka used the familial term Tato, referring to Burian Hordiyenko as the head of the entire crime family on the northeastern coast.

"I cannot make that decision right now. We can't move forward with any business until we put our current crisis to bed. I do not relish the idea of going to prison, or worse, disappointing Burian." He owed his adoptive father everything, and the thought of not living up to his expectations caused a searing pain in Volodymyr's chest. He gestured for Mishka to sit in the matching leather wing-back chair facing the fire. "What news do you have for me regarding the Benningtons?"

Mishka crossed the carpet and took the offered seat. "We still have no information, sir. However, one of your Kaptains had an idea. We were complaining about how our teenaged daughters are always on social media, and Ivan ordered us to monitor the Bennington girl's Instagram, Facebook, Snapchat, and TikTok accounts."

Volodymyr's blood stirred, and he sat up, leaning toward Mishka. "And?"

"Nothing so far. But Ivan thinks it's possible that the girl checks her social channels but just isn't commenting. You know how teenage girls are."

Volodymyr narrowed his eyes. "No, I can't say that I do."

"Well, if she's anything like my daughter, she's online constantly. It's probably killing her not to be able to talk to her friends. We grounded our Olena from her phone, and you'd have thought the house would collapse from her screaming."

Volodymyr side-eyed Mishka and rotated his pipe to keep him going on the point.

"Sorry, sir. But it's highly likely that the Bennington girl is watching her friends through their posts."

"If she's not posting, how does that help us?"

"Ivan has set up a fake account with a profile photo of a beautiful young woman. Since her closest friends are dead, he'll start by following friends of friends of Melissa Bennington's boyfriend and liking his posts. Gradually, he'll make his way into the closer friend group. We might draw Melissa out of hiding if she's jealous of this new, gorgeous girl flirting with her boyfriend."

Volodymyr eased back into his chair and puffed his pipe, letting the earthy tobacco smoke float from his mouth upward and inhaling it for the second time through his nose. "There are many ifs and maybes in your plan, and it sounds like it will take a lot of time. Time is not something we have."

"I understand that, sir. But at this point, Ivan's plan is our only hope."

"You must be careful. If we've thought of monitoring her social media, certainly the police have too. Take care they don't find you before we find her."

After school, Kendall returned home with her brothers to find their parents arguing, as usual. Their mom turned when they came in the door, and she rushed to Joey. "The school called to tell me you were fighting with other boys at recess." She held his face in her hands and inspected his nose. "You don't look much worse for wear, but what do you have to say for yourself?"

Kendall's little brother shrugged, and pulling away from their mom, he stared at his shoes.

"Answer me, young man."

"Brett Anderson started it." Joey then recounted the playground fight.

"There is not to be any fighting. Now go straight to your room. You're grounded for a week."

Joey clomped toward the hall, but on his way, Jack held out his fist to bump Joey's in a congratulatory manner before he grabbed a basketball and took off out the front door. Kendall followed her little brother, seeking refuge from her parents in her room. Her parents may as well have grounded her too, as much time as she spent hiding out in her room. Kendall cringed as her parents started up again. She learned her dad got a job, but he wasn't happy with it. He had to start at the bottom of the seniority list, and it would take years for him before he was making a decent wage. Her mother yelled back that she was tired of listening to his complaining. At that point, Kendall put on her headphones and shut her parents out.

She listened to her favorite playlist while she opened Instagram on her phone. Scrolling, she paused to watch the first few seconds of a funny cat video and then two others showing the silly antics of puppies. Several of her old friends posted pictures of themselves in fancy dresses at the homecoming dance. She smiled, though her heart stung with loneliness at her friends' fun night. Then tears formed in her eyes when she saw Fletcher's slideshow of images. The first few pictures in the series were innocent enough. She could have believed that Fletcher and Delaney went to the dance as friends. But by the end of the collection, there was no denying that Fletcher was no longer thinking about Kendall.

Hot tears blurred images of her boyfriend with his hands and mouth all over Delaney Finch. Quickly, she moved to Snapchat and TikTok to see if there were more pictures of them. She thumbed over to Facebook to read any comments there. A post of Fletcher kissing Delaney announced that he was in a new relationship. Before she thought, before she even knew what she was doing, she clicked on an angry face emoji, and she threw her phone down on her bed.

Kendall buried her face in her pink, fuzzy pillow and cried into its softness. Her real life, the one from before, was truly over. And she had no life here, in the present. She couldn't sit by and watch Fletcher fall in love with someone else. Kendall had to let him know she was still alive. Still watching. Still wanting him. If only he could wait for her until she testified at the trial, or even until she was eighteen and could make her own decisions about where she lived and the risks she took. She believed Fletch would wait for her if only he knew.

Sitting up, Kendall reached for her phone. She scrolled back through Fletcher's feed to find images of her and him together. Thankfully, he hadn't removed them yet. That proved he still loved her, didn't it? Kendall chewed on her chapped lower lip. What if she sent Fletcher a direct message? No one else could see personal messages, right?

She wiped the moisture from her eyes and pressed on the messenger icon and typed. "Fletch, it's me! I'm alive. I'm using a fake profile name, so no one can tell it's me. I saw the pictures you posted from homecoming. And though it makes me sad to see you with Delaney, I forgive you for taking her. But please don't give up on us, Fletch. If you can just hold on, we can be together again. I love you, and I know you love me. Please, Fletcher, I can't look at any more pictures of you and Delaney. Wait for me."

Kendall stared at her message while static short-circuited her nervous system. Her finger hovered over the send button. Should she post it? Could she?

ANGER MIXED in a toxic cocktail with embarrassment and caused Teresa's breath to come fast as she pressed her foot heavily on the gas pedal. She had received a call from Tomas's school principal who informed her that her son had been in a playground fistfight during lunch recess. Teresa had to share the story with Emory so she could leave work early to pick Tomas up from school. Her boss had given her a look of pity, which sat like a cannon-ball in Teresa's gut. She didn't need sympathy. She could handle her son and his troubles on her own, just fine.

Teresa pulled into the semi-circular drive at the front of the school. Tomas waited for her by the flagpole. He avoided meeting her eye as he trudged toward her car. Opening the door, he tossed his backpack on the floor before he got in.

"I can't believe you, Tomas Luis Mendez! We've talked about fighting, before."

"I know, Mom. I tried to avoid it. But when Brett grabbed my shoulders, I chop-blocked him like you taught me. It made him let go, but then he hit me in the face. I didn't start it, I swear! Then Joey tackled him, and Brett punched him in the nose. It's all Brett's fault."

Teresa's body stilled, and she drew in a deep breath. "Joey Miller was involved, too?"

"Yeah. He stood up for me."

Thoughts raced through her mind. "Let me see your eye." She inspected her son's bruised eye socket. There had been no actual fights before Joey Miller enrolled in the school. "Let's get you home and put some ice on your eye. You're going to have a real shiner by morning."

"You think so?" The excitement in Tomas's voice reignited her anger. "Can I call Dirk?"

"This is not something to be proud of, young man."

Tomas dropped his chin and clipped in his seat belt. "Okay. But all I did was try to get Brett off me."

Teresa sat with a mixture of the pride she'd warned Tomas against and feelings of dismay. She was glad her son had used the self-defense technique she'd taught him. But it hadn't been enough. Maybe she should enroll him in a martial arts course where he could learn both follow through moves that would prevent getting socked in the eye, and more importantly, how to avoid a fight in the first place. It was times like these Teresa wished Tomas had a father in his life. Perhaps she should let him call Dirk.

21

At midnight, Dirk and Hank sat in Dirk's black Rubicon at the crest of Old Mill Hill which stood sentinel over the trailer park housing Chance Bergman's girlfriend. They'd confirmed her address after their first night of surveillance and learned the home belonged to a woman named Pricilla West.

Tonight was the night Ziggy informed them that Bergman was supposed to show up for his pre-arranged conjugal visit. The trailer community was small, and from their vantage point, Dirk and Hank were able to see any cars approaching the neighborhood. Dirk never knew if he could trust his CI or not. But so far, his information had been good enough times to make the stakeout worth the time and risk.

Dirk and Hank weren't alone on the midnight watch. Four other sheriff's deputies were parked in two unmarked cars in other hidden locations throughout the small neighborhood all waiting for the dangerous fugitive's arrival.

Dirk sipped the last drops of his lukewarm coffee. "Got any more of that gerbil food?"

Hank rummaged in his backpack and pulled out a pack of trail mix. He tossed it to Dirk. "Think Bergman will show tonight?"

"No telling. But it's worth a shot. It's not like you and I have any better places to be." Dirk poured a fistful of snack into his hand. They sat in silence for another forty-five minutes. The only sound was their mutual crunching on nuts.

Dirk's phone buzzed, and he lifted it to see Emory's image glowing on the screen. "Yeah, Boss, what's up?"

Emory's voice floated into his ear and wound down into his chest. "How's the stakeout going?"

"No action so far." Dirk wished he could have this conversation in private. It was awkward enough talking to Emory these days, and even more so when he had an audience.

"How long will you stay out there if Bergman doesn't show?"

"Until dawn, I suppose. My informant is usually reliable. I don't doubt that he heard what he said he did. Ziggy identified Rogers as one of Bergman's men who he heard talking about him. We saw Rogers talking with the woman we think is Bergman's girl here, yesterday. So, Ziggy's story lines up. But of course, that doesn't mean Bergman didn't change his plans."

"And you're sure the girlfriend is home, now?"

"Yeah, we watched her arrive presumably after work about three hours ago and she hasn't gone anywhere since. Her living room light is on. She's probably waiting up for Bergman. At least that's what I hope."

"Well, I wanted to see if you'd like to come over to my place when you're done with your mission. It doesn't matter how late. You still have a key, right?"

Dirk's gut knotted up at her proposal. On one hand, he wanted nothing more than to spend the rest of the night with Emory. But on the other, the desired action came with some serious implications. He didn't want to communicate anything he couldn't back up. "I doubt I'll have time."

"Tomorrow's Saturday. So, even if you aren't free until morning, you could still come." Her silky tone caused his heart to pound.

He eyed Hank and turned away slightly, dropping his tone. Hank took the hint and popped his Air pods into his ears. Grateful, Dirk continued, "I don't think we should go there right now, Em. It's better if we slow things down, don't you think? I don't want you to get hurt."

Emory said nothing for a moment, and then her voice came over the line as soft as velvet. "I don't believe for a minute that it's *me* you're worried about getting hurt. I think you're trying to protect yourself. Either way, we need to talk this through. Ignoring me—us—won't make any of this go away."

A flush of heat exploded in Dirk's belly, throwing flames up his throat. "I showed up to talk to you the other night. *You're* the one who walked away. As far as I'm concerned, that says everything."

"Dirk, I—"

"Hold on a minute, Chief. A car's approaching."

Headlights appeared at the entrance to the trailer park, soon followed by a second pair. Hank popped his ear buds out and sat forward, raising night vision binoculars to his eyes. "We've got activity down below."

Dirk peered through the windshield and watched as the truck they saw the night before, and another car rolled up the main street of the neighborhood. "Gotta go, Chief. I'll call you later." He ended the call. The vehicles stopped in front of Pricilla West's trailer. "They're not even trying to make this hard." Dirk chuckled. "Come on kid, let's head down there to give the local boys some backup." The minute he said that his police radio crackled to life.

"Suspect has arrived, but he's not alone. There's a driver in the truck with him, and three more men in a second car."

Dirk pressed the button on the radio microphone. "Stand down. Let's wait them out. It's been a while since Bergman has seen his girl. I don't think it will take long for him to send his buddies packing. We'll go in and grab him once they leave. Hank and I are on our way down the hill on foot. We'll meet up with you in a few."

After turning off his engine, Dirk pulled on his coat and glanced at Hank. "Bundle up, sweetheart. It's colder than the North Pole out there."

Hank slid a black beanie over his blond hair. "Too bad we can't just watch from up here in the comfort of the warm car."

"No way. I'm not missing out on any action." *At least not at work,* he thought wryly. "Let's go, kid."

The partners crept down the hill on foot and hopped

over a barbed wire fence that marked the edge of the trailer park property. Bending low, they moved behind the line of trailers on the opposite side of the street from Bergman's destination, their boots crunching softly on the frozen grass. When they were parallel with the girlfriend's trailer, they cut in between two homes toward the street and crouched behind one of the sheriff's deputy's unmarked cars. Their breath puffed white plumes into the frigid night.

Dirk tapped on the passenger side window. The deputy rolled it down. Dirk whispered, "Make sure your dome light is off, then let us in. It's freezing out here."

The officer did as Dirk asked and then popped open the lock on the doors. Carefully, Dirk opened the back door, and he and Hank slid inside, gently closing the door behind them. "Were you able to positively identify that one of those men is Bergman?"

"We think so, Sir. We're almost certain the big guy riding shotgun in the truck is him, but we can't be one hundred percent certain."

Hank checked the magazine on his weapon. "Guess we'll just have to wait and see." He snapped his rifle back together.

Dirk unzipped his North Face coat in the heat of the running car. "We'll wait here with you."

One of the deputies offered Dirk and Hank Twizzlers from a half-empty bag on the seat that had scented the cruiser with a sickly-sweet odor. Dirk shook his head, but Hank helped himself to two. An hour later, the front door of the trailer opened, and four of the five men exited.

Dirk chuckled. "Called it! None of those guys are

Bergman. He's staying inside for his booty-call. Once he felt safe, he kicked his buddies out."

The deputy zipped his coat. "Looks like this is going to be an easy nab and grab."

Dirk checked his weapon and felt for the two spare magazines he carried with him. "Don't get complacent. That's when things go wrong."

One of the men exiting the trailer shoved another down the stairs causing him to fall. Swearing, the assaulted man leapt to his feet. Dirk pressed the electric lever and lowered his window enough to hear the argument.

"What the hell, Arno?" The man reached up and with both hands, grabbed the coat collar of the man who pushed him, and threw him down. "You want to go?"

"Any time!" Scrambling to his hands and knees, the man called Arno sprang up toward the other and tackled him. The men wrestled on the frozen ground until Pricilla West flung the trailer door opened and stepped out on to her small porch wearing a glittery crop top over her ample bust and a hot pink micro skirt that barely covered anything.

She yelled, "Stop fighting, you morons! Be quiet before somebody calls the cops." Neighborhood dogs barked in the distance at the night's disturbance.

Bergman followed Pricilla out and looped his arm around her waist. His hand boldly reaching up inside her top to grope her breast. "Get the hell out of here before I shoot your dumb asses. God damn it! You're interrupting us, you stupid bastards!" He waved a pistol in his free hand and his men scattered to their vehicles and drove away.

Dirk and his team waited for fifteen minutes after the four men left the house to slip out of their cars and creep toward the front door. While Dirk and the lead deputy armed with a no-knock warrant, held their weapons at low-ready and approached the entrance, Hank and the second deputy ran to cover the backside of the aluminum structure in case Bergman tried to escape out of a window.

Though they weren't required to announce themselves, the deputy yelled, "Police!" as he reared back and kicked in the door. No sooner than his foot hit the flimsy hollow-core than a shotgun blast ripped through the thin trailer door, blowing it apart in a shower of wood and metal splinters. Spatter slammed into the deputy's chest. His vest absorbed most of the hit, but the force sent him sprawling backward off the porch.

Dirk had no time to check on the fallen deputy before a second blast tore through the thin wall next to the door near where he stood. He dove from the porch, straining as he flew to see if the deputy who'd been blown off his feet, was still alive. Heat from the shot seared his face. His stinging jaw letting him know he had likely caught a stray pellet. He brushed at the pain with his shoulder as he rolled to his knee and leveled his Glock at the door.

"Give it up, Bergman." Dirk yelled. "We've got you surrounded, and there's only one way out of that place."

The man inside cackled. "Nope, it's *we* who have *you* surrounded! For a much-needed fix, a little birdie named

Zig Zag told me you'd be calling. You're screwed, Deputy Marshal!"

The car they had watched drive away returned, this time with all four men inside. They fired rounds at the law enforcement officers as they passed. Dirk turned and rolled across the ground, returning fire as the sedan rolled by. His shots blew out a side window hitting one of the shooters, and shredded a back tire, but the car kept going. Another shotgun blast tore a second hole in the trailer wall.

Pricilla's shrill voice screamed from within, "Chance! Stop it! You're ruining my house. It's all I have!"

"Shut your suck, bitch. I'm the one what pays the bills 'round here." A third random spatter blasted through the side of the structure.

Dirk darted for cover behind the neighbor's car. He couldn't make it to the fallen deputy without getting himself shot too. He called for backup. "We have an officer down. I don't know his status, but he is unresponsive." Dirk then spoke to Hank. "Flannigan, take cover. Help is on the way."

"Roger that."

Once the sedan was completely past them and Dirk was sure Hank was safe, he crept toward the fallen deputy. As quickly as he could, he worked to get the man out of harm's way. More shots echoed into the night. There was no time to waste. With adrenaline-powered strength, Dirk rolled the deputy over his shoulder and fireman-carried him to his position behind the car. Bergman's henchmen turned around to make another pass. They fired their weapons randomly into the yard and surrounding trailers. Dirk prayed that no innocent people were hit.

Quickly and efficiently, he checked over the deputy's body. Dirk felt for a pulse in the man's carotid artery. A weak flutter pulsed against his fingertips. He was alive! Thankfully, he'd been wearing body armor. More than one of the scattershot pellets had found their mark outside of the officer's Kevlar, but he would live. "Help is on the way, man. Stay here, where you're safe. I've got to go."

Dirk saw Hank and the second deputy dive behind a rusted-out VW van two doors down. Bullets from the returning car riddled its old body with hollow-sounding *thunks*. Hank peered around its rounded tail-end and lined up his shot for the next time the sedan rolled by. Dirk made eye contact with him and gestured his plan with hand motions.

The car turned at the end of the road and was on its way back toward them. Dirk sprinted to the back side of the trailer Bergman was hiding in and crouched low to the ground. Meanwhile, Hank, taking careful aim with his M4 Carbine, waited for the car to return. As it rolled past, Hank squeezed the trigger. The driver's head snapped to the side. The car veered off course, its tires squealing as it slammed into an empty car parked on the street.

Dirk murmured, "Two down, three to go." Hank had been an expert shooter in the Army, and Dirk knew it was only a matter of time before the others in the car would either surrender or meet their fate. He waited, and after a barrage of their gunfire lit up the inside of the car, Dirk heard precisely two more rifle shots. Hank gave him a nod and a stiff-fingered wave to move forward.

Dirk peered through a gap in the thread-bare curtains covering a large window at the rear of Pricilla's trailer. Bergman stood in the center of the living room, facing the entrance. He cocked his shotgun and braced himself to use it. Dirk eased a few steps to the side so he could see what remained of the front door. What was left of it hung from a single warped hinge.

He signaled to Hank, who fired a round into the flagging door to distract Bergman. The flimsy wood splintered into dust. Simultaneously, Dirk used the sound of Hank's rifle blast to cover the noise of striking the trailer's rear window with the handle of his gun and the resultant shattering of glass.

As Dirk had hoped, Bergman reacted to Hank's shot at the door with another burst from his shotgun out the opening of the blown apart entryway. Dirk took advantage of the split-second distraction to climb in through the back window. He landed on the broken glass, aimed his weapon, and fired. Bergman collapsed where he stood, crumpling over his shotgun. Pricilla screamed from somewhere at the front of the trailer.

Clearing the few back rooms as he moved steadily toward the front room, Dirk kept his Glock level and ready. When he found Pricilla, he waved her toward the gaping hole at the front of her home. "Pricilla West is coming out," he yelled. "Hold your fire!"

As the woman made her way to what used to be her front door, Dirk kicked Bergman's shotgun away from his body. He crouched down to feel his neck for pulse, when the man he believed to be dead, grabbed hold of his arm and yanked him off balance. Dirk used the momentum to roll over the top of the man hoping to land on his feet. Bergman swept his leg across the floor catching Dirk's boots before they gained purchase. Dirk fell to his knees but was able to raise his gun.

The shriek of a banshee sounded behind him one second before Pricilla's arms wrapped around his neck. She flung her weight against him, knocking him to the side. Bergman pulled a knife from a scabbard on his belt and lunged toward Dirk's chest.

Dirk rammed his elbow into Pricilla's body, dislodging her long enough for him to steady his gun with both hands just as Bergman's knife sliced through the front of Dirk's coat. Every third round in Sterling's Glock was a hollow point. This played in his favor when the HP round entered Bergman's orbital cavity, mushroomed through his cranium, and caused instant death. Bergman's knife clattered to the floor as he breathed his last.

Pricilla screamed and scrambled toward the door. Hank who was coming in, pulled her through and passed her off to the deputy behind him. He bolted through the door. "Dirk!"

"I'm okay." Hank sprinted to his side and checked him over. "I said I'm okay. How's the deputy who got shot?"

Hank pressed the microphone on his vest. "We're clear inside." He held out a hand to help Dirk to his feet. "He's alive. His partner is with him waiting for the bus to get here."

Sirens sounded in the night, and Dirk rubbed the

tense muscles at the back of his neck. "How about the men in the crashed car? Any survivors?"

"One. The deputy is cuffing and mirandizing him now. They had a shit-ton of weapons in that car, Dirk. We got lucky."

"No luck about it." Dirk narrowed his eyes as he studied his partner. "What happened to your face?"

"It's nothing." Hank brushed at his skinned cheek. "Probably shouldn't dive headfirst when taking cover behind a hippie van." The kid grinned. "What happened to yours?"

Dirk touched the burned spot on his jaw. "Nothing. Probably shouldn't stick out my chin when someone is shooting at me." He clapped his partner on the shoulder. "Let's get this mess cleared up and get out of here."

22

———

Hank sat in the therapist's office in one of three blue tweed chairs that faced each other. This was the last place he wanted to spend his Saturday morning, but he had made a commitment to Amy to work on their marriage. At the beginning he tried in earnest, but since then things had gone even further south. He panned his gaze around the room across the therapist's desk, the coffee service on the sideboard, and the bland medical office artwork hanging on the wall. Amy was currently recounting everything he ever did wrong in the first year of their marriage. Her list went way back to when he was in the Army—to a time, in his memory, they didn't have any of the problems she claimed.

He ran his fingers down the crease of his slacks and tugged at the crisp white collar of his button-down shirt. He tuned back into his wife's diatribe for a few seconds, enough to find that she had moved past their Army years —during which he remembered them being in love and having fun—and she was now regaling their therapist, once again, with his failures as a husband since he'd become a Deputy US Marshal. Hank took a deep breath and released it as quietly as he could so that neither of the women in the room could interpret it as confrontational or passive-aggressive in any way.

Hank and Amy had been in therapy twice a week for two months, and nothing was changing. At least not in a positive manner. Hank didn't think Amy felt better, no matter which of the therapist's suggestions they tried. She had them practice communication skills, conflict resolution techniques, and he'd worked hard to express appreciation for his wife. All of which seemed productive during the sessions but fell flat on their face when he and Amy were out in real life.

Amy had been asking him for a divorce for a while now. Maybe he should just let go and give it to her. She'd worn him down.

The therapist broke into Amy's monologue, which drew Hank's attention. "Amy, I am a marriage counselor, and that's my specialty. That being said, I would like to recommend that you see a psychiatrist. I believe you may suffer from clinical depression, and I think it might even be helpful for you to test for bipolar disorder."

Amy sputtered in shock, and Hank sat forward, taking her hand in his. He looked askance at their therapist. "What makes you think Amy could be bipolar?"

"I'm not qualified to make such a judgment, which is why I am referring Amy to a medical doctor. I have a couple of psychiatrists whom I can recommend, or you may like to find your own. That, of course, is up to you."

The therapist closed her notebook and sat forward. "Amy, you wrestle with severe mood swings. The stimulus that you describe in our sessions rarely warrants the extreme emotional reactions that you have. I believe you would receive greater help and relief by seeing a medical professional."

Hank was of two minds. On one hand, he agreed with the therapist and felt as though someone finally saw what he had been experiencing for the past couple of years. But on the other hand, a surge of protectiveness flared in his chest. On a strange level, he wanted to defend his wife and her behavior. Surely, he was to blame for some of the trouble.

Amy yanked her fingers away from him. "You think I don't have a right to be upset about how dangerous Hank's job is? Look at his face! He was in a shootout just last night! Would you want to raise a child with a man who insisted on putting his life at risk every time he went to work?"

Hank self-consciously touched the raspberry scab forming on his cheekbone. How did Amy know he'd been involved in a shooting? He filled his cheeks with air and blew it out. She had probably seen something on the news. "Amy, Joanne isn't saying you should have to live with my job. She's not saying anything about me at all. She's concerned for *your* health. And I am too. I think we should table any talk of divorce until you have a chance to speak with a psychiatrist and have some tests done. I could move back into the apartment and take care of you, if you want. None of this stress and anxiety can be good for the baby." Amy glared at him, and he turned to the therapist. "Couldn't her mood swings be because of the pregnancy? I read that pregnancy hormones can cause that."

"Yes, of course. That's a distinct possibility. And one thing we've learned over the years is that both pregnancy and postpartum hormonal shifts can cause serious, and sometimes debilitating, depression. I'd like to make sure Amy is seeing a doctor who can care for her needs, if that's the case." She faced Amy. "This type of depression can be dangerous for a baby in utero as well as once the baby is born. It isn't your fault, and we can help you. But you need to be seeing the correct doctor. Does all of this make sense?"

Amy crossed her arms over her chest and glared at both Hank and the therapist. "No. It does not make sense! It feels like you two are ganging up on me, telling me I'm crazy. You're right about one thing, though. None of this is my fault. It's having to live with Hank and his adrenaline addiction that is driving me insane. If you were listening, I just explained that to you. Again!"

"No one's ganging up on you, Amy." Hank rested his hand on her knee, but she pulled away. He sat back and considered the woman he had once been head over heels in love with. But the person before him hardly resembled her. "I'm concerned about you, and I'm concerned about you taking care of yourself during your pregnancy, *and* after." He couldn't bring himself to say out loud that he was worried that she might harm their baby. Emotional exhaustion pressed down on his shoulders. Weariness seeped into his bones, and he felt helpless.

"My mother will take care of me." Amy let out a sigh.

"I guess I agree we don't need to go through this stress of divorcing until after the baby is born. But I'm still going to have my attorney get everything prepared. I can't live with you anymore, Hank. Your lack of concern for me and our baby is untenable."

Hank stared at the woman he was married to. It had become impossible to talk to her. Impossible to reach her. In her mind, every discomfort she'd ever faced was his fault, and she accepted zero culpability for her own actions. There was no reasoning with her at all. It seemed as though she'd completely forgotten their wonderful early years.

Perhaps she *was* bipolar, or at least depressed. He wondered if there were any medications that she could take during pregnancy that would help her stabilize but that would be safe for the baby. But what if she took too much? His gaze drifted to Amy's rounding belly. Regardless of the mother, he loved the little life growing inside her and would do everything he could to protect it. It occurred to him then that he might need to petition for full custody if Amy didn't do the things she needed to get better—before the baby was born. At the very least, he ought to be prepared.

That evening, Hank sat with Dirk watching football on TV. Hank was grateful that his partner let him stay at his house while his personal life was in such turmoil. He also appreciated that Dirk didn't expect him to talk about his troubles unless he wanted to, and that he could just enjoy their friendship without pressure.

Hank's phone dinged with a text, and he glanced at the screen. It was a message from Amy's mom. A video from his mother-in-law's house played of Amy opening a large, gift-wrapped box. Alarm jolted his heart, and his pulse raced as he watched the reel. An icy flush of concern washed through his body for a few seconds as he sorted through possible holidays he must have missed. Was it Amy's birthday? No, her birthday was in March. Thanksgiving wasn't a gift-giving holiday.

In the video, Amy unwrapped and opened the top of the box. Dozens of pink balloons floated up to the ceiling. She squealed with delight and bounced happily on her toes. The video ended, and a text arrived.

Amy's Mom: Thought you might want to know you're having a little girl.

Hank tossed his phone onto the coffee table and jammed all ten fingers into his hair.

Dirk watched him for several seconds before muting the game. "You, okay?"

Shrugging, Hank combed back his ruffled hair. "I guess. I mean, I should be happy. I just found out Amy and I are having a girl."

"Amy texted you?"

"No. Her mother did. She sent me a video of a gender reveal party I obviously was not invited to. I guess her mom had enough compassion to let me know."

In typical fashion, Dirk didn't rush into commenting. He sipped his beer and gave Hank time to settle his emotions. "I'm sorry you had to find out that way, but congratulations. You're going to be a great dad. That little girl is going to wrap you so tightly around her finger you won't be able to breathe." Dirk sent him a half grin.

"Yeah. I just need to concentrate on her." Hank cocked his head and smiled. "I'm having a little girl!"

The friends tapped beer cans and Dirk unmuted the TV. Hank leaned back against the couch, not really watching the game. Instead, he tried to imagine what it would be like to raise a daughter on his own.

23

At the end of the day, Joey went to his cubby at the back of the classroom to get his coat and backpack. Tomas gathered his things two sections away. "Hey, Tomas, want to come over to my house after school to play?"

Tomas frowned. "Nah. I can't do anything after school." He scuffed the toe of a worn tennis shoe on the tile floor. "My mom works, so I have to go to after school care, every day." Then his eyes brightened, and he stood a little taller. "But I asked my mom if you could come over to our house on some Saturday. She said maybe, but she'd have to meet your parents first."

"Cool! I'll ask my mom, too."

"Here." Tomas wrote his mom's phone number on a scrap of paper with a red crayon.

The boys stood together in the line to leave the classroom. Other kids who rode the school bus lined up first, then the kids who went to after school care, and finally those who lived close enough to the school to walk home.

The friends waved at each other when it came time to split, and Joey made his way outside to the sidewalk. He looked down the road to the right to see if Kendall or Jack were coming, but neither of them were there. Now that his parents were more comfortable with the neighborhood, they allowed them to walk home on their own.

Joey pumped his fist when he didn't see his brother and sister because he planned to stop by the 7-11 to meet the man who owned the store. Brett had told him that whenever he and his friends stopped by, the owner gave them candy. Joey wanted in on that deal.

The 7-11 was a block away from the road he usually walked down. But it was on the corner, and he could see it from the schoolyard. He glanced one more time over his shoulder to check for his brother and sister before he turned toward the store. Jack would probably agree to go with him, but there was no way Kendall would let him wander from their regular path home. With no siblings in sight, Joey gripped the straps of his backpack and ran down the street to 7-11.

The parking lot needed re-paving. Dried weeds filled the cracks in the worn asphalt. Joey jumped over a frozen puddle and stepped onto the concrete walk at the front of the store. He yanked open one side of the double glass doors. An electronic bell sounded when he went inside, and country western music played through the speakers in the ceiling. It seemed like every store they went into in Montana played that kind of music. He had never heard it before... when they lived in their old house.

A man with graying brown hair who seemed about the same age as Joey's dad sat on a stool behind the counter, watching something on an iPad. He looked up at the bell. "Well, hello there," he greeted. "I haven't seen you around here before. Are you new to the neighborhood?" The man's smile was friendly, and it put Joey at ease.

"Yeah, we just moved here."

"My name is Mr. Grant, and this here is Fang." The man patted the scruffy head of a black, shaggy dog who got to his feet to meet Joey.

Joey loved dogs and knelt to let Fang lick his face. The dog's warm tongue tickled his cheek and neck, and Joey laughed. He looked up at Mr. Grant. "I'm Joey Miller. I like your dog."

"Seems he likes you, too." Mr. Grant smiled, showing a gap between his two front teeth. "Do you go to Big Horn Elementary School?"

"Yeah." Joey giggled as the dog slathered his face. "A boy at school named Brett said you gave candy to kids."

Mr. Grant chuckled. "Sometimes. Why don't you pick your favorite candy bar from the shelf as a 'welcome to the neighborhood' gift from me?"

"Gee, thanks!" Joey panned the shelf filled with colorful wrappers while he stroked Fang's velvety ears. It was hard to choose only one from so many options. He finally settled on a packet of peanut butter M&Ms. Fang tried to pull the candy from Joey's fingers.

"OK, Fang. That's enough." Mr. Grant slid his fingers into Fang's collar and pulled him back. "Looks like you've made a new friend already. Want to give him a dog treat?"

"Sure!"

Mr. Grant reached into a box of dog snacks that

looked like bones he kept under the counter and held it out for Joey. "Tell him to sit before you give it to him."

"Sit, Fang." Eyeing the treat, the dog obeyed, wagging his curly tail across the floor behind him. Joey gave him the morsel.

"You'll be his friend forever, now." Mr. Grant placed the box back where he got it. "Where are you from, Joey?"

"Ridgefield, Connecticut." As soon as the words left Joey's lips, fear swooped through him like a mockingbird defending her nest. Joey clapped a hand over his mouth. He wasn't supposed to tell that secret to anyone. Ever.

Mr. Grant's eyebrows crunched together, and he narrowed his eyes. "Are you all right?"

Joey's legs felt twitchy, like they wanted to run. "I gotta go." He darted to the door, pushing it open. He took a quick second and called back, "Bye, Fang!"

Nerves fueled Joey's sprint all the way to his house. He burst through the front door and slammed it behind him, his chest heaving.

His mom was on the living room couch, talking on her phone. She murmured, "I have to go." Her eyes widened as she set the device on the cushion next to her, and she stared at him. "What on earth is going on? You charged in here like someone was chasing you. Where are your brother and sister?"

"I don't know. They didn't walk me home."

"Well, take off your shoes. Don't track dirt across my clean floors."

Joey dropped his backpack on the floor under the coat tree and kicked off his sneakers. "Hey, Mom? Can I play at my friend Tomas's house next Saturday?"

"The weekend after Thanksgiving?"

"I guess."

"We'll have to see. Where does he live?"

Joey shrugged. "He said his mom has to meet you first. Here's her number." He pulled a wadded-up paper from his jeans pocket. Luckily, the smeared crayon numerals were still readable. "Will you call her right now?"

24

Days later, Kendall walked home after school with her brothers. The autumn sun was warm on her face even though the temperature was a chilly twenty-four degrees. Idly, she wondered if it would snow over Thanksgiving break. Jack had taken to carrying his basketball with him everywhere he went, practicing his dribbling moves. The constant echoey sound of rubber bouncing off the sidewalk was super irritating. They were still blocks away from the park when he took off toward the basketball court and his new friends waiting for him there.

Kendall patted Joey's shoulder. "Why didn't you go to the park with Jack?"

"He never lets me play with them," her little brother grumbled. He stopped on the sidewalk and looked up at her. "Kendall, are Mom and Dad getting a divorce?"

She sighed, releasing the tension that flared up her neck with his question. "I don't know, buddy. But don't worry. You know that you, Jack, and I will always have each other. Right?"

"I guess."

A black panel van raced up the street, screeching to a stop next to them. Hot spikes of adrenaline pierced Kendall's scalp, but before she could move, the back door flew open. A thick man dressed in gray track suit jumped out. They'd found her! Alarm's clanged in her head. She dropped her backpack and tried to run. The man held a knife in one hand, and he grabbed hold of Kendall's arm with the other, yanking her toward the vehicle. Frantically, she screamed and scratched at her assailant's face, twisting back and forth trying to pull away from his fierce grip.

Joey grabbed hold of her coat and tried to tug her away from the man. "Jack! Jack, help!"

Smokey breath heated her ear. "Stop fighting, or your little brother will come too."

Kendall's body shuddered at his threat, but she struggled against him anyway. Their shouting got the attention of their brother and his three friends, who sprinted toward the van. Jack was the first one there. "Let go of her!" He chucked the basketball, hitting the man in the head and causing him to drop his knife. His friends joined the fray, hitting and shoving the attacker away from Kendall.

Jack's friend, Tanner, landed a punch to the man's face causing him to stumble to the side. "Get off her, you perv!"

Jack threw his arms around Kendall's waist and yanked her free. "Run, Kendall! Somebody call the cops!"

The man lost his balance along with his grip on Kendall, but still he struck at Jack's head and torso. Jack pivoted and gave him a side-kick to the chest. He fell backward into the van. Tires squealed. The would-be kidnapper almost fell from the vehicle as it raced away, but he reached out, grabbed the door handle, slamming the van door shut. One of Jack's friends jumped on his bike and raced after the van. When the driver realized he was being followed, he swerved, almost hitting the boy and forcing him into a row of bushes at the side of the street. The vehicle raced away, leaving the acrid scent of burnt rubber which made Kendall's eyes water. She and Jack had tumbled to the ground. Her chest heaved and her limbs trembled.

"Are you okay?" Jack gripped her shoulders and helped her to her feet, looking her up and down. He threw his arms around her. "I've got you, Kendall. You're safe."

Through heavy puffs of breath, the boy who chased the van said, "There was no license plate. I chased them as far as I could, before they ran me off the road."

"Thanks, dude. Are you okay?" Jack kept an arm around Kendall.

"Yeah, just some scratches. That's all. Who were those guys?"

"I don't know, but we need to go home and tell Mom and Dad. They'll want to call the cops."

Kendall grasped for Joey, who stood behind her sobbing. Her heart stampeded through her chest. If her brothers and Jack's friends hadn't been right there, she'd be inside that van careening toward her death. "Come here, buddy. It's okay. You guys saved my life!" The three siblings clung desperately to each other as all the kids hurried to the Miller's house.

"Mom! Dad!" Jack yelled as they rushed through the door. "Some guy just tried to grab Kendall off the street and force her into their car!"

The blood drained from their mother's face, and her hand flew to her chest. "Your dad's at work." She stared at the children. Her head swung back and forth, and she looked like she was in shock.

Jack took command. "Mom!" He gave her a gentle shake. "You need to call the cops!"

"This wasn't supposed to happen." Their mother seemed unable to snap out of it.

"I know, Mom. But it *did*. You call 911. I'll call Deputy Sterling. Where is his phone number?" Jack left their mom to rummage through a kitchen drawer. Finding the business card he needed, he dialed the number on her phone.

Kendall collapsed onto the couch, wishing her mom would stop staring into the distance and instead wrap her in her arms for comfort. Tears built up in Kendall's eyes and flowed down her cheeks, a precursor to wracking sobs. "I'll never be safe. They won't stop until they kill me!" Kendall had never experienced such fear. Not even when she witnessed the murder of her friends, and she had been way beyond terrified then. But the realization that the killers had likely found her and would keep trying to kill her until they succeeded chilled her to the bone. Worse was the fact that her family could be murdered too, just for being near her.

"Yeah, Chief Grey?" Jack moved down the hall so his friends in the front room couldn't hear, but Kendall listened to his whispers. "This is Jack Miller, you know, from the family you're supposed to be protecting?" Jack's voice wobbled as he took charge. He explained what had happened and then nodded several times. "Okay. Please, hurry!"

Their mom's color returned to her cheeks. "What did she say?"

Jack returned to the living room. "She said to lock all the doors and stay together. They're on their way." Jack dashed to the front door and threw the deadbolt. "Mom, check the back door. Did you call the cops?'

"Not yet. I'm still not sure what happened."

Red rage filled Jack's face. With the phone still in his fist, he punched a hole into the drywall. "What is the matter with you?" He yelled at their mom. Blood seeped from his injured knuckles, and he shook out his hand. "Everyone go downstairs. We'll wait for the police there." He darted through the kitchen and locked the back door.

Kendall took Joey's hand and ran with him to the stairs. Jack and his friends followed their mom down. Together, they huddled in the corner of the basement behind the furnace. Joey was trying hard to be brave, but tears streaked his chubby cheeks. Kendall pulled him close and stared at her mom, hoping she would offer comfort to him, too, but she seemed unable.

Glaring at their mom, Jack held the phone out to her. "You should call Dad, don't you think?"

25

Dirk typed with two fingers as he finalized his report of their apprehension and arrest of Chance Bergman. It was always gratifying to bring in a fugitive, but even more so when the guy had shot at cops. Dirk was proud of the work they did the previous Friday. Considering the potential firepower they had faced, the fact that the only injuries were those sustained by the deputy whose bruised sternum would hurt like hell and keep him out of work for weeks—that and Hank's skinned cheek—it was a miracle.

Speaking of Hank, his partner walked into the office late without his usual upbeat greeting. He tossed his navy peacoat on the back of his chair and slumped into the seat.

"What's up, kid?" Dirk swiveled to face him.

Hank clicked on his computer. "Nothing. I just got off another irritating phone call with Amy. What's going on here?"

That explained why Hank was late—and his bad

mood. The kid had been so hopeful when he and Amy had started counseling, but it wasn't going well. "I'm finishing up my report on the Bergman case. Otherwise, it's been dead. Teresa took an early lunch, and the chief has been holed up in her office all morning."

Hank glanced at their boss's closed door and then returned his gaze to Dirk. "I think it's truly over between me and Amy." Dirk kept his expression even and waited for Hank to continue when he was ready to. "Last weekend, our therapist recommended Amy get some tests from a psychiatrist. She might have some serious issues, which on one hand gives me a little relief that I'm not imaging her unstable behavior, but on the other scares me since we're expecting our baby in a few months. You know?"

Dirk steepled his fingers and wondered how best to help his partner. "And after your call with her today, you're thinking of granting Amy a divorce?"

"Well, as you know, it's not just after today. It's been adding up. I don't see us ever overcoming the mess we've become. And I don't think I even want to try anymore."

"That's a big decision. One you don't want to make emotionally. Maybe you should take the rest of the day off. Go to the range or watch a movie. Get your mind off things for a while."

"Yeah, maybe." Hank propped his elbows on his desk and pressed his face into his hands. "I need to find a good divorce attorney. One who can help me gain custody of the baby. I'm scared about Amy's mental condition."

"It'd probably be good to get some counsel, but some of what she's going through might be hormonal, too. I'd wait and see what the psychiatrist says before launching the custody grenade."

"Don't you think I should be worried?"

"I didn't say that. I think you're right to be concerned. Just don't overreact before you need to, that's all."

Hank crossed his arms on the desktop and rested his head on them.

Emory's door swung open and banged loudly against the wall behind it. Her stunning green eyes flashed with concern as she flew out of her office. "Two men in a black panel van just tried to grab Kendall Miller off the street near their home. Jack and some of his friends helped fight them off. The kids got away and are home safely. But I can't help but wonder if the would-be kidnappers were sent from Kovalenko's crime family. If they know where the Millers live, the family is in great danger."

Dirk's pulse rocketed with the news. He jumped to his feet and grabbed his jacket. "We're on the way. Did they give a description of the van to the police?"

"I think we were the first call they made. I'll call 911. You guys get over there."

"Come on, Hank. This ought to get your mind off your troubles. Let's go." Hank followed him, and they ran toward the elevator. They were fifteen minutes from the Millers' house. That was an eternity if the mobsters attacked. If it was someone else, they still needed to hunt down the van to keep other kids safe from some roaming sicko.

Dirk's Rubicon screeched to a stop on the road outside the Miller's home. He and Hank jumped out of the vehicle and ran to the front door. They knocked. After no answer, they tried the knob. It was locked.

Dirk yelled, "US Marshals. We're coming in!" Hank slammed his shoulder against the door. The frame split, giving them access. They ran inside, yelling. "Kendall? Ann? James?"

The partners drew their guns and began to clear the house. Dirk checked the bedrooms, stopping at the hole in the wall. He pointed it out to Hank. Dirk's adrenaline spiked. He figured someone violent was already in the house. Hank searched the front of the house. After they gave an all-clear signal to each other, they made their way toward the basement door.

Standing on either side of the access, they softly opened the door. When no shots were fired, they crept slowly down the wooden stairs. At the halfway point on the steps, they saw Ann huddled together with the six children in the corner behind the furnace.

Jack peeled away from the huddle. "Was it the Ukrainian's? Have they found us? Is that why those men tried to grab my sister?"

"Hey, calm down. Did someone you don't know enter the house?"

Jack was red-faced and breathing hard. "No. I locked the doors."

"Good. Smart move. You are safe, now. Let's go upstairs." Dirk directed the young man to the steps. Hank waited for the rest of the frightened group to mount the stairs. Once everyone was in the kitchen, he closed the basement door behind them. Dirk led them to the living room. Kendall sat next to her mother on the couch. Jack paced and his friends huddled together near an armchair. Joey sat cross-legged on the floor in front of them. "First of all, Kendall, are you alright? Are you hurt in any way?"

The pretty girl shook her head and absently rubbed her wrist. "I'm not hurt. Thanks to Jack and his friends." She shared a look with her middle brother before tears flooded her eyes and she pressed her face into her mother's shoulder.

Dirk rested a calming hand on Jack's back and the young man stopped treading back and forth. "Sounds like you saved your sister's life. Can you tell us what happened?"

Jack looked like he might cry, but he ground his teeth together and answered. "I didn't see the whole thing. I was on the basketball court in the park when I heard Kendall scream. Joey was tugging her coat to get her away from a man who was pulling her into the back door of a black van. I ran to help. I threw my basketball at the man who had grabbed Kendall and then we fought him off. He hit me a couple of times before he lost his grip on Kendall. Then he fell back into the van, and it peeled away. That's pretty much all I know."

Hank took notes on his phone. "A black panel van. Do you know what make? Did you see a license plate?"

Jack gripped his hips and shook his head. "I'm not sure about what kind of van, but I know there was no plate because Jason chased it on his bike. They drove him off the road before they disappeared."

Dirk shifted his gaze to Jack's friend. "Is that how you got the scratches on your face?"

"Yeah."

"Did you give a description of the car to the police?"

Ann cleared her throat. "I did. Chief Grey called and told me to call them, and when I did, I told them exactly what Jack just told you."

"Okay, good." Dirk glanced around the room. "Where is your husband? Is he on his way home from work?"

"Oh," Ann looked mildly startled. "In all the excitement, I forgot to call him."

"I'll check in with the police while you get ahold of him. I'd feel much more comfortable if we kept eyes on all of you right now. We can't be certain this is a threat from New Jersey, but I'd rather be safe than sorry." Dirk slid out his phone. "Can any of you kids describe either of the men? Or did you notice anything that might help us identify them?"

KENDALL SAT up as her mother pulled her arm away from Kendall's shoulders. Taking her phone with her, her mom went into the kitchen to call their dad. Kendall turned to answer Deputy Sterling. "I saw the man who grabbed me, but not the driver. I can try to describe him, but I didn't recognize him. He wasn't one of the men who... who killed my..." She tried not to cry, but pressure built up in her chest and behind her eyes, and she couldn't finish her sentence.

Deputy Sterling sat on the coffee table across from her and took her hands in his. "It's okay, Kendall. You are incredibly brave. Whatever you remember will be helpful."

"He had dark eyebrows that met in the middle. And he had a tattoo on his neck. Just black ink. A symbol or something. I'm not sure what it was."

"Okay. That's good. Can you guess how tall he was? Was he heavy or thin?"

"He was taller than us. Maybe six feet. And thick."

"Did he say anything to you or Joey? Or maybe to the driver?"

Sniffling, she answered, "I don't think so."

"Joey? Did you hear anything?"

Her little brother's eyes were as wide as baseballs. "The man who grabbed Kendall yelled, 'Go! Get us out of here!' when he fell into the car."

Deputy Flannigan knelt next to Joey. "Good job remembering. Can you tell us what his voice sounded like?"

"Not like my dad's. It was different, kind of. Funny sounding."

The deputies shared a look, and Kendall wondered if *funny sounding* meant Ukrainian. "Do you think they found us? Will we have to move again?" she sniffled.

The dark-haired deputy answered, "We don't know yet. But we'll stay with you until we do. You're safe." He gave her hands a reassuring squeeze. Sirens sounded in the distance. The police were on their way.

Her mother yelled something on her phone from the kitchen, and Kendall's cheeks heated. Jack took the seat on the couch next to her. Embarrassed by her mother,

Kendall glanced at the two marshals. "They've been fighting a lot lately," she explained. "I think it's the stress."

Joey piped up. "And my dad wants to be married to a different lady."

Shocked her little brother would share something so private, Kendall yanked on his arm, pulling him closer to her. "Joey!" she chastised. "We don't know that. Don't repeat things you aren't sure of."

"I *am* sure." He shot to his feet. "I told you. I heard dad say he wanted to be with that other lady named Mindy. He said he was gonna leave his wife and be with her."

Ann shouted from the other room again. "This was not supposed to happen! You promised!"

The deputies exchanged glances, and Sterling touched Joey's shoulder. "Joey, did you hear your dad talking to someone from Connecticut on the phone?"

"Yeah. It was Mindy. She's a lady who used to work for him."

Her mom came around the corner from the kitchen. "Sorry about that. James is on his way home now."

Deputy Sterling nodded, acknowledging her mom's statement and waited for her to sit. "Have any of you, besides James, been in contact with people from your past?"

"Absolutely, not." Her mom crossed her arms over her chest.

Jack shook his head, but Joey fidgeted and dropped his gaze to the floor.

"Joey?" Deputy Sterling leaned down to look at his face. "Have you talked to anyone?"

Kendall's little brother shrugged. When he looked up tears dripped from his eyes. "I accidently told the man at 7-11 that we used to live in Connecticut. Is it my fault they found us?"

"What man?"

"The owner." Joey sniffed.

The deputies exchanged glances, and the blond one pulled out his phone and left the room. Sterling gently squeezed Joey's shoulder. "We'll look into it. Anyone else?" His dark eyes met Kendall's, and she glanced away from his scrutiny.

"I haven't talked to anyone, but..." It sickened her to think that her curiosity may have put her family's lives at risk. Again. "I sometimes look at my old friends on their socials."

A muscle in the deputy's jaw bulged. "We talked about that, Kendall."

"I know, but—"

"There are no buts. The rules are in place to keep you safe. I doubt Joey's slip was a problem, but you and your dad both broke the rules. Either one of you could have led the mob to find you."

Her mother stood and paced in front of the picture window. "Could have? Do you think there's a chance that the kidnappers aren't from the mob?"

"It's impossible to know unless we catch them. The local cops will put out an APB on the van. Hopefully, they'll find those guys and get them off the streets, whoever they are."

The blond deputy returned. "The chief is getting in touch with the FBI Cyber Crime Unit to dig into Kendall's social media accounts. Hopefully, they'll be able to tell if anyone else has been snooping around."

Four police officers arrived in two cruisers. Deputy Sterling met them at the door. After giving them a quick briefing, he sent them out to canvas the neighborhood. "Ask if anyone saw anything. Check for Ring cameras. There may be tire marks in the street, too."

One of the female officers held up a bag with a knife inside. "We found this in the street. Did the kids say the suspect had a weapon?"

Dirk looked at Kendall and Jack. Her heart leapt. "Yes! I don't know why I forgot that. The man held a knife and told me not to fight him or they'd take Joey, too."

"Run that for prints. And keep me posted."

26

Emory coordinated the search for the men in the van and the investigation into Kendall Miller's social media accounts from her office. She also asked for a warrant to delve into James Miller's phone records to see if there was anything nefarious going on with him. As far as she could ascertain, those were the only two possible avenues through which the Ukrainians could have located the Millers. The abduction attempt could be completely unconnected, but that didn't make her feel better. The cops needed to find that van.

When Emory received the text from Dirk assuring her that the Miller family was safe and secure, she felt she could finally leave the office. Teresa was packing up her things for the day when Emory stepped out of her workspace. "Teresa, do you have time to grab a cup of coffee or something before you head home today?"

Her friendship with Teresa was a new one. Emory spent so many hours at work she had no extra time to make friends outside of the office. She dated someone from work, and her only friend was another deputy marshal. She knew this wasn't healthy, but it was her life. There simply wasn't room for anything else. Mostly, she and Dirk had been able to manage their work and personal relationships, and she hoped the same would be true with her friendship with Teresa.

"Yeah, sure. I don't have to pick up Tomas until six. I'd love to grab a cup of something."

"Great!" The tight muscles in Emory's neck and shoulders released slightly, knowing that Teresa seemed to want a friendship as much as she did. "I'm getting ready to leave now. Dirk and Hank have everything under control at the Millers' house. I just need to call Captain Furman at Billings PD and ask for an around-the-clock police presence at their residence until we're certain the attempted abduction didn't stem from the Ukrainian crime family in New Jersey."

"Okay," Teresa pushed her arms into the sleeves of her puffy winter coat. "Why don't we meet at that new coffee shop on 17th? I've heard it's a pretty cool place."

"Sounds good. I'll be right behind you as soon as I make the call." Emory returned to her office and dialed the police chief. He agreed to post a squad car at the Miller residence for the next forty-eight hours and then they would reassess the need. Emory was comfortable with the plan because if the trouble came from the Kovalenko family, they would know it by then.

Emory gathered her things and slid into her forest-green wool coat. Standing in the center of the empty office, she panned her gaze around the space. Her eyes rested on Dirk's desk. Even though she saw him every day, she missed him. She longed for the easy way they were with each other before the night she brought up wanting to have kids with him. For the past several weeks, she had reflected on which she wanted more—Dirk or children. Emory knew she had to make a choice. If she chose to have a baby and left Dirk, she'd never find a man she cared about as much as she loved him. Maybe there was a way to assuage her desire for children that didn't involve birthing her own. But when she tried to go down that road in her mind, her heart ached. She wanted both Dirk and children and didn't want to live without either of them. It was a horrible decision to make, like choosing which hand you'd rather lose. And the worst thing was she had no one she could talk to about it besides Dirk, and he was in the middle of it all.

She let out a deep sigh, turned out the lights, and locked the office door behind her. Spending time with Teresa was exactly what she needed, only she didn't know how much of her personal business she should share. Dirk and Teresa had been coworkers and friends for much longer than she and Teresa had. Not to mention that Emory was chief of the team, which put her in an awkward situation where work friendships were concerned. The lines were blurry, and her loneliness was profound. She was determined to feel her way through it.

Emory opened the door to the new coffee shop and entered a warm room filled with the scent of freshly roasted beans and baked goods. Her stomach rolled in anticipation. Jazz notes thrummed gently from hidden speakers, loud enough to hear but soft enough for conversation. The lighting cast a warm glow over intimate seating vignettes. Emory could see why the new shop enjoyed such rave reviews.

Teresa waved at her from a table for two in the back corner next to a gas fireplace blazing cheerfully. Emory raised her hand in acknowledgment and then pointed to the counter. She ordered a large London Fog. A strong tea latte would give her the boost she needed.

When her drink was ready, she joined Teresa at the table. "I love this place! It's so cozy."

Teresa sipped her drink. "I've heard lots of good things about it. And I can see why. The coffee tastes great too. How's yours?"

"I have tea." Emory snapped the lid off her cup and blew the steam away, cooling it slightly before she took a sip of the creamy drink. "Hmm, that sure tastes good. Thanks for meeting me here."

"I'm glad you suggested it. We haven't had a lot of time to visit, and I've been wanting to talk to you about Joey Miller and Tomas. It's a topic that crosses from work into my personal life."

"Yes. How's that going?"

"Well, it appears the boys are going to be friends, whether I like it or not." Teresa laughed softly. "A couple days ago, the third-grade bullies were picking on Joey and Tomas stepped in. Tomas came home with a black eye, and I heard Joey received a bloody nose. Thankfully, the school principal allowed them a first-time warning. If it happens again, they'll get suspended."

"Oh, no! What's your take on all of that?"

Teresa pursed her lips. "I'm proud of Tomas for standing up for Joey. Of course, I'd rather the boys didn't come to blows. But I think my son did the right thing. The incident certainly solidified the friendship between them. Tomas has been begging for Joey to come over to play. I guess I'd rather they were at my house than at the Millers. At least I know they'd be safe." Teresa took a thoughtful sip. "I just don't know where the lines are. I'll have to tell the Millers that I'm a deputy marshal, but do I confess that I know their family situation? It seems like a gray area to me."

Emory took a thoughtful sip of tea. She knew all about the fuzzy lines between work and personal lives. "They may feel relieved. They'd know their son has a friend he can be safe with. Does Tomas know we're working with Joey's family?"

"No. And I wouldn't want him to know. First of all, it goes against the whole point of WITSEC, and second, that's too much responsibility for a nine-year-old kid."

"I agree. Perhaps it would be better if you said nothing and just let their friendship develop naturally." Emory stared into the hot milky liquid in her paper cup. "It is a vague area. It seems like I spend most of my time wading through various hues of gray lately." She shifted her gaze to Teresa and considered her next words. "My relationship with Dirk, yours and my friendship, even the stuff going on with Hank—as Chief, I should keep the boundaries crystal clear, but we're all in each other's lives. Sometimes it feels very tenuous."

"It could be. But we're all adults and good people with the best of intentions for each other. I think it will be okay. Besides," Teresa grinned, "who else are we supposed to hang out with? None of us has enough personal time to meet other people."

Emory laughed. "Sadly, that's completely true." She reached across the table and squeezed Teresa's forearm. "I'm glad we're friends."

"Me too. And since we're friends, I have to ask, what's going on between you and Dirk?"

This was where the lines got even more murky. Emory needed someone to talk to, but was it wise to share her personal relationship drama with someone else at the office? "I don't know how much I should say. I guess if I talk to you purely about my own issues..."

"Emory, I don't want you to talk to me about anything that makes you feel uncomfortable. But I give you my word that whatever you share with me will stay between us."

"Thank you." Emory hesitated for another long moment before she dove in. "You know that Dirk and I took that road trip together several weeks ago. Well, I thought we were becoming serious... probably moving towards marriage. I think it's fair to say that Dirk was in that same place emotionally. That is, until I mentioned really wanting to have a family. I'll spare you the details but suffice it to say that Dirk does not want children. So, we seem to be at an impasse. Neither of us wants to leave the other, but we can't move forward, either.

"And making matters worse, my parents are coming to Thanksgiving dinner next week at Dirk's place." Emory closed her eyes and covered her mouth with her hand.

"So? I'm sure they'll get along," Teresa encouraged.

Emory took a fortifying breath. "I've given my parents

the impression that Dirk and I are planning a future together. My dad is a Marine Corps General, and I know without a doubt that he has researched Dirk's entire military history. I also know my dad will expect Dirk to speak to him about his intentions. It's all a big mess now, and I'm not sure what to do."

"Crap. That's a tough situation." Teresa turned her cup in circles. "The good news is that Dirk is a standup guy. No matter what. If he needs to talk to your dad, that's what he'll do."

Emory smirked. "That's what worries me."

"It's too bad—what happened to Dirk. It was sad enough that his baby died. But then his ex-wife really screwed him over. I'm sure you know the story." Emory nodded. "He's so good with kids. I rely on him, maybe too heavily, to be a positive male influence for Tomas. I know Laurie Dillinger does the same thing for her son. Dirk would make a great dad. I think he's just protecting himself, don't you?"

"Absolutely. But there's no talking him out of it."

"No, I don't suppose there is. What will you do?"

Emory chewed her bottom lip. "I have to pick between sharing my life with Dirk or having a family, but I don't know how to choose. I asked him if he'd consider other options, like adoption, but he is too afraid of the risk. For Dirk, it's love that's risky."

"I suppose, but there's always hope. After all, he swore he'd never fall in love again, either. But here you are. You are the first woman he's dated more than twice since Hannah left him. Maybe he just needs more time."

"Maybe, but I don't have a lot more time. I'm not in my twenties anymore, you know."

27

————

Teresa had agreed that Thomas could invite Joey to come over to play on the Saturday before Thanksgiving. She much preferred that the boys come to her house where she could keep an eye on them. It was hard knowing the inside story of a family who was unaware of her insight. Guilt nibbled at her conscience, but she knew Tomas would be safe at home. She did not have the same confidence in him playing at Joey's.

It was nine o'clock and her son was still in his pjs watching cartoons. "Tomas, you need to get dressed. We're not leaving here until your room is clean, so if you want to have your friend over, you better get moving!"

Tomas gave her no indication he heard her, so Teresa found the remote control and clicked off the mindless show. "Get dressed and clean your room!"

He groaned and dramatically rolled off the couch. "Okay, I'm going!"

After they did their house cleaning chores and had

gone to the grocery store, Teresa drove Tomas to the Miller's house. Together, they went to the door.

Joey's mother answered the knock by peering through the slim window parallel to the entrance before she opened it. "Hello! You must be Tomas, and Mrs. Mendez?"

Rather than getting into a long explanation of why she was not "Mrs. Mendez," Teresa smiled, "Please, call me Teresa."

"Hi Teresa. I'm Ann. It's nice to meet you both. Joey's been bouncing around the house all morning. He's so excited to play with you, Tomas." Ann dropped her voice and spoke directly to Teresa. "Honestly, I'd rather the boy's play here, if you don't mind. We had a scare last week. You may have heard about the men in a van that tried to grab a girl off the street? That was my daughter. I'm feeling like I want to keep my kids close by."

"I heard about that, and to be honest Ann, I heard about it from my work before I got the notice from the school. You see, I'm a Deputy US Marshal from the Billings office. You already know my co-workers Dirk Sterling and Hank Flannigan."

A look of suspicious confusion swept across Ann's face. "Oh. Yes, I do. Is this whole thing part of your job? Are you keeping an eye on us?"

"No, that isn't it. I was aware that Joey attended school with Tomas, but the boys became friends on their own. I admit, I was hesitant about letting them build a friend-ship, too. But I decided to stay out of their way."

Ann hesitated. "Well... I guess Joey couldn't be in a safer home, than yours."

"I assure you they will be safe."

"Okay, then... Thanks for picking Joey up."

"It was no problem. I was out running errands anyway."

Joey tugged on his coat and burst out the door, jumping off the front porch, and landing the lawn. "Joseph Miller!" Ann chastised. "Get back here and say hello to Tomas's mother."

The boy reluctantly walked back to the porch. "Hi."

Teresa laughed at both boys' exuberance. "Hi, Joey. I'm Teresa. You boys go ahead and get some of that energy out before we get in the car." She turned back to Ann. "Let me give you my phone number and address." The moms exchanged contact information.

Tomas and Joey chased each other around the yard playing some ruleless-version of tackle-tag. Both mothers watched their sons, and Ann lowered her voice. "I know the boys got into a bit of trouble last week. But I appreciate your son standing up for mine. It's hard to be the new kid at school."

"I don't like them fighting, but sometimes the best way to stop a bully is to stand up to him. I'm just glad they didn't get suspended."

"They were lucky."

"Indeed. What time would you like Joey home?"

"My husband has some errands to run this afternoon. He'll probably finish around four o'clock. Why doesn't he stop by and pick Joey up around three?"

"That works." Teresa called the boys to her car, and they waved at Ann as they drove away.

Tomas and Joey bolted to her son's room to pull out all his toys. Teresa enjoyed hearing their laughter from the kitchen. After putting away the groceries, she stirred together ingredients to make Tomas's favorite peanut butter-chocolate chip cookies. She brewed a cup of tea to sip on while she waited for the treats to bake. The warm scent of melting butter and sugar gave comfort to her afternoon, and relaxing, she picked up a long-neglected novel.

The boys brought their favorite toys, superhero action figures and Legos out to the living room. Teresa listened to their chatter while they played.

Joey pushed two blocks together. "Tomas, where's your dad?"

Tomas shrugged. "Don't have one."

Teresa's heart twisted as though someone had wrung it out like a wet rag. The truth was Tomas was better off without the man who had fathered him. Once again, she was filled with gratitude for Dirk's influence in her son's life, and she absently wondered how he and Emory would work things out.

The timer buzzed. "The cookies are ready. Come get some while they're warm," Teresa called. She poured both boys a glass of milk.

Joey took a big bite of cookie. "It's okay if you don't have a dad. My sister says we probably won't have one either pretty soon."

Teresa's ears perked up. Tomas gulped his milk and

wiped the residue from his upper lip with his sleeve. "How come?"

Joey's face wrinkled in thought. "He talks to some other lady all the time who used to work for him when we lived at our old house. I heard him tell her he was going to leave my mom and marry her."

Tomas's dark eyes widened. "Does your mom know?"

"I dunno. I don't think so. Want to play outside?"

"Yeah! I have a cool swing set. Let's go!" Tomas crammed the rest of his cookie into his mouth and the boys grabbed their coats and dashed outside.

Teresa's mind raced with the information she had overheard, the most concerning of which was that James Miller was in contact with someone from their old life. This went directly against WITSEC protocol.

She found her phone and dialed Emory.

DIRK ALREADY KNEW that James Miller had been mixed up in dangerous indiscretions, and he decided it was time to call the man and insist they meet. He'd heard a version of the story from Kendall and Joey already, and he figured it was time to set James straight. They agreed upon a sports bar on the outskirts of town. James was there already sipping a pint at the bar, when Dirk entered the darkened hoppy-smelling pub.

He eased onto the stool next to James. "Miller." Dirk ordered an IPA on draft.

James acknowledged Dirk with a nod. "I'm still not used to being called that. What's up, Deputy Sterling?

Why the secret meeting? Have you found some information about the men who tried to kidnap my daughter?"

"We have the knife he threatened her with in evidence, and the cops found the van stripped and burned out down by the river. But that's all so far. But our concern is that you've compromised your family's new identities. Any idea how that could have happened... *James*?" Dirk's jaw hardened in distaste. He had no respect for a man who put his entire family at risk for an illicit love affair.

James leaned back and regarded Dirk. "Why does it sound like you think this is my fault? I thought it was the job of the US Marshals to keep us safe."

Dirk glared at him. "Here's the thing, Miller. No witnesses in the history of WITSEC who have followed the rules of the program have ever come to harm. It is our job to protect you as long as you follow the rules. So, you tell me. Is there any reason you can think of that your location could be compromised?"

The smaller man squirmed under Dirk's scrutiny. "I don't know what you're talking about. How would I know?"

"You're telling me you don't remember any middle of the night phone calls to a woman who lives in Connecticut? A woman who used to work for you at your investment firm in New York?"

Miller's eyes widened, and his mouth hung open. "Did you tap my phone? I still have a constitutional right to privacy, you know."

"No, we didn't tap your phone. And you may have a right to privacy, but isn't your family's right to safety a little more important than that? Their right to stay alive? A man almost kidnapped your daughter, James. If Kovalenko's family has found you, we might not be able to keep you safe. You may have to change locations again. Is all of that worth a piece of ass?"

James stared at him for a long minute before he covered his face with his hands and shook his head. "Nothing's more important than my family's safety, but Mindy isn't just a piece of ass. I love her. We love each other. You have no idea how hard it is to live with a woman like Ann. Before this all happened, Mindy and I were planning on getting married. I was going to tell Ann I was leaving her, but then all hell broke loose. What am I supposed to do, Sterling? What would you do in my place?"

Dirk drew in a long swallow of beer. "For starters, I would never step out on my wife." He took another drink, hoping to rid his voice of the bitterness swelling in his throat. "Not to mention risking the lives of my children. This isn't a game, Miller."

The man beside him seemed to deflate. "I know that. But what do I do? I can't live a lie on top of a lie in my own house for the rest of my life. I love Mindy, and I need to be with her."

"Let me explain to you what that might look like. You could get a divorce from Ann, and we could set you up with a new identity in a new location and even bring your girlfriend into that situation. Especially if your phone calls to her have brought the Kovalenkos to your door, because that means you've put your girlfriend's life at risk now, too." Dirk shook his head in disgust. "It would also mean you would never have contact with Ann or any of your children—ever again. You would still pay child support and alimony, but the US Marshal system would distribute the funds. Is this woman worth that level of sacrifice?"

Blood drained from James's face. He pressed his fingertips into his eye sockets and rubbed. When he opened his eyes again, he nodded. "Yes, I think she is."

"Are you sure she's going to feel the same way about you when all you can offer her is a meager income and a home somewhere in middle America? Remember, she fell in love with a wealthy man. Just think. If she ditches you, you'll be on your own with no family."

One side of Miller's mouth curled up. "Don't worry. Money won't be a problem."

What the hell was this character up to? Dirk narrowed his eyes. "For the time being, you need to have a conversation with your wife. Do not make any more phone calls to your girlfriend. And whatever you think you have going financially—stop doing it. Don't doubt that Kovalenko can find you through what you *believe* to be hidden money. Stop being so stupid, Miller. Your children's lives depend on it."

28

<hr>

For the first time since Hank and Amy separated, she had agreed to meet him for dinner. He picked her up at her mother's house, and they rode in his truck to the restaurant. He chose a spot on the backside of the building to park, and he backed in.

"At first, I thought dinner would be a good idea." Hank unclicked his seat belt and turned to face Amy. "But honestly, I don't have much of an appetite, and what I have to say might be better said in private."

Amy crossed her arms over her chest and looked at him with suspicion glinting in her eyes. "What is this? A bait and switch?"

"Not intentionally. I just don't want to discuss our personal business in public. That's all."

"What do you have to discuss that we haven't talked about in our therapy sessions?"

Hank pulled in a deep breath and held it for several seconds before letting it out in a whoosh. "I'm ready to grant you the divorce you asked for." Tears pricked his eyes as he spoke words he thought he'd never say. "The more we try to fix things, the worse they get. I think we're finally at an impasse."

Amy's face turned red, and her eyes widened before she narrowed them to a slit. "What the hell are you talking about, Hank? I can't believe you! After all of this... and now when I'm pregnant... you want to divorce me? How dare you?" Amy shrieked. "Is there another woman?"

Confused, Hank drew back. "Of course, not. Calm down. I don't think you getting so upset is good for the baby." Amy's inconsistency of thought disturbed him deeply. Her mood swings gave him emotional whiplash.

"Maybe you should have thought about that before you announced you want a divorce!"

Hank consciously calmed his breathing, much like he did when he was firing his long-range weapon. Rash emotions would not help the situation. When his heart rate stabilized, he said, "If you recall, Amy, you're the one who asked for a divorce. I didn't want one. At the time, I believed we could make it work. But now, I no longer think that. I'm only agreeing with what you've been saying all along."

Amy grasped for his hand, and he let her hold it. "But I didn't mean it, Hank! I was only trying to get you to see how serious I am about you quitting your job. I can't live with worrying about you all the time whenever you're not home. And I don't think it would be fair for our children either. I was just trying to get you to understand. Please don't leave me, Hank!"

Her words punched him in the gut. Was Amy saying

she never really wanted a divorce? She had just been manipulating him? That was even worse! His stomach knotted up so tight he thought he might be sick. "I can't believe you. I can't believe you would try to trick me like that!" Hank stared at her, his head shaking in disbelief. "Well, your games didn't pan out the way you hoped, did they? I tried for months to make things work out, only to realize we don't have a future together. If I was uncertain before, I'm more than convinced now. I'm sorry our marriage turned out this way."

"You son of a bitch! I can't believe you're thinking of leaving me, your pregnant wife! What kind of horrible person are you?" Amy's hand flew up, and she struck his face, stinging his scabbed-over cheek.

Everything she did, from the way she spoke to him to her slap across his face, confirmed what he had come to know in his heart. Amy needed help to get mentally healthy, but he couldn't be part of her journey any longer. "I can see that you're upset, and I'm sorry. I didn't want this. But here we are. I hope you will talk to one of the doctors that our therapist recommended and get better. I want that for you. As for me, I've been staying with Dirk this whole time, but now I'll need to find a permanent place of my own with room for the baby."

Amy's face twisted with fury. "If you think I'm going to allow you to spend any time with my baby, you're crazy!" Amy struck out at him again, but this time he caught her wrist and prevented her from hitting him.

"The court will decide how much parenting time we each get. But the judge *will* allow me time with our baby, and I want to be prepared to do so. That's all I'm saying."

"You're going to take me to court?" Tears and snot dripped down her face. She looked like a wild animal as she clutched at his arms. "Please don't leave me, Hank! We can fix this. I know we can."

He pried her fingers from his arm and pushed her hands back to her lap. "It's too late for that, Amy. I'm sorry. But the only future I want to have with you will involve organizing childcare." Hank truly hoped she could get healthy, but until she did, he planned to appeal to the court for full custody. She was too unstable to care for herself, let alone an infant. Of course, telling her that now would only make matters worse. "I've said all that I came to say tonight. Do you have anything to add? Or shall I drive you home?"

"I thought you were taking me to dinner." The desperation in her eyes caused him to pity her.

"I think sitting across the table with each other tonight would be miserably uncomfortable for us both. I know you need to eat, though. Would you like me to order you something to go?"

"Hank, please don't do this. I'm scared. How will I take care of the baby on my own? You're being incredibly selfish."

Hank dialed the restaurant and ordered a steak dinner to go. He tossed his phone onto the console. "Change is scary and so is having a baby. But that's not a reason to stay in a miserable marriage with someone you don't love. We'll figure it out." He opened the truck door and hopped down. "I'm going to go grab your dinner, and then I'll take you home."

They were silent on the way back to his mother-in-law's house. He parked at the curb, and when Amy turned to him, fury shot from her eyes. "I hate you, Hank Flannigan! The next time you hear from me it will be through my lawyer." She got out of the truck, and snatching the bag with her dinner, she slammed the door so hard the truck shook.

Hank watched as she stormed toward the house. He was miserable. All his hopes and dreams of a loving family were walking away from him. Yet with his next breath, he felt free.

29

Thanksgiving morning, Emory arrived at Dirk's house with her parents in tow. They had arrived in Billings the night before and slept in the spare room in her apartment that she generally used as a home office. Luckily, she had a bed stuffed in the room along with her desk and computer equipment. It was good to see them, though inevitably her parents treated her like she was still seventeen, not as a full-grown woman with a successful career and a mind of her own.

Emory parked on Dirk's gravel drive behind his Rubicon. "Here we are!" She took a deep breath and held it for a few seconds before releasing it. Nerves skittered up and down her spine and zipped down her arms and legs to her extremities. She would have been nervous to introduce Dirk to her father in any situation, but with Dirk and her not knowing where they stood regarding their future together, it was all that more awkward.

Her dad, who rode in the front passenger seat, bent

his head so he could view Dirk's entire house through the windshield. "Nice place. I'm looking forward to meeting your Marine, Emy-Sue."

"Dad! He hasn't been in the Marine Corps for over ten years. Please do not treat him like he's under your command. And please, please, don't call me Emy-Sue in front of anyone!"

"Once a Marine, always a Marine, darlin'. If he's the man he ought to be, he won't have any trouble with it." Her father climbed out of her car and opened the back door for her mother.

"Mom, make him behave. Please!"

Her mother patted her hand and smiled. "Your father is just being protective. That's his job. I'm sure there's nothing to worry about."

"Not other than my pride. Besides, I don't need protecting. I'm a grown woman. You guys know that, don't you?" She said to her mother's back as the door closed behind her. Groaning, Emory got out of her car and clicked her fob to open the trunk. "Dad, will you please help me carry some of this food?" Her father looked minorly irritated at being distracted from his primary objective. But he acquiesced and hauled in the bulk of the food that Emory brought for the dinner.

Without knocking, Emory opened the front door and called out, "Happy Thanksgiving! Where shall I put all this stuff?" She led the way to Dirk's kitchen and found him checking on the turkey roasting in the oven. "It smells amazing in here."

Dirk closed the oven and turned to kiss Emory's cheek. Glancing beyond her and seeing her parents, he set the turkey baster on the counter and wiped his hands on a towel. "Welcome, General Grey, Mrs. Grey. It's an honor to have you in my home." He held out his hand to the general.

Emory's father studied Dirk for the longest set of seconds she had ever experienced before he accepted Dirk's hand. "Thank you for the invitation. We've been looking forward to getting to know you."

"As have I. Can I get you both something to drink?"

"Since it's before noon, I'll settle for an iced tea. Elaine?"

Emory's mother brought her usual softness to the conversation with her gentle southern accent and charm. "Tea would be lovely, thank you, Dirk. It's wonderful to meet you. You have a beautiful home. We're so happy to be here. And please, call me Elaine."

Emory offered to get the drinks so Dirk could continue tending the food. As she poured, her father's voice barked at Dirk. "Your hair is a bit longer than regulation, don't you think, son?" Emory's shoulders bunched. *Here we go*, she thought.

But Dirk laughed at the comment. "Yes, sir. It definitely is. But in my defense, it's cold up here in Montana. It's nothing like the heat of the sandbox."

"Sounds like you need to toughen up, Marine." Her dad chuckled.

Henry chose that moment to join them. He had quaffed his blonde bangs up in their usual standing swirl above his forehead.

Dirk pointed at Henry with a wooden spoon. "At least I don't have to go to the beauty parlor to have my hairdo done." He laughed. "I leave that to my Army brother here. Sir, this is Henry Flanagan, my partner. I call him Hank, or Kid, for short. Hank, these are the chief's parents, General and Mrs. Grey."

Her father shook Henry's hand. "Nice to meet you, Army. I suppose you're here to clean up any of our leftovers?"

"Yes, sir." Henry's handsome smile flashed. "I know what picky eaters you Marines are. I don't get how you jarheads ever survive in country."

The three men laughed, and her father clapped Henry on the back. Emory always marveled at the instant comradery, the inner service rivalry, and the friendly jabs that went on between members of the various military services. Henry led her parents into the living room to watch football on TV while everyone waited for dinner to cook.

Teresa and Tomas arrived at the same time as Laurie and Caleb, and the noise level instantly tripled. Emory could no longer monitor the embarrassing things her father was saying, so she poured herself a glass of wine and made small talk with the other ladies.

Laurie joined her in drinking wine, but Teresa opted for a beer. "Hey boys," she called out to the kids. "Why don't you two put on your coats and go out back to play? I'll call you when dinner's ready." She rolled her eyes at Laurie. "I can't even hear myself think with all their ruckus."

"Maybe they'll burn off some of that energy before they have to sit still for the meal." Laurie crossed her fingers and laughed.

The women helped Dirk organize all the food, plugging in crock pots and prepping serving dishes. Emory joined Dirk at the stovetop, where he whisked the gravy. She slid her arm around his waist. "I apologize ahead of time for any uncomfortable thing my father says."

He bent to the side and planted a kiss on top of her head. "Stop worrying about it, Em. I like your dad. And your mom. You look just like her, you know. Without the southern accent."

"I can always turn it on if you like. I did grow up primarily in the South."

"Oh yeah?" His dark eyes warmed. "That could be sexy. Why'd you lose the drawl?"

Emory chuffed. "It's hard enough to be taken seriously as a blonde woman as it is. I would never have made it through the academy if I spoke like my mother."

Teresa poked her head between them. "What are you two whispering about over here?" she teased. "Hey, real quick, I wanted to talk to you guys before we all sit down at the table. It's about Joey Miller."

Emory and Dirk turned simultaneously to face her. "Has something happened?"

"Nothing involving the case." Teresa recapped the story of the playground bullies for Dirk. "I already told the chief about this, but I thought you should know, too."

"How did the other kid make out? I hope Tomas popped him a good one."

"Dirk, that isn't helpful."

"It's the only way to stop a bully, T."

She pursed her lips at him. "Either way, the incident

sealed the boys as fast friends, and I agreed to have Joey over to play last Saturday."

Emory touched Teresa's arm comfortingly. "Are you worried about them fighting at school again?"

Dirk grinned at them. "They're just boys being boys, ladies. I'm sure it's nothing to worry about."

"I agree, Dirk. I'm not concerned about that, but there is something else. I'm not sure if the chief told you this, but when Joey was at our house, he talked about how volatile it was at their house. It doesn't sound like things are going well with the Millers."

"No, it isn't." Dirk agreed. "Hank and I learned a lot about their situation last week when Kendall was almost grabbed off the street. It looks like James and Ann might be heading for a divorce."

Teresa sighed. "That poor little boy. He's just being tossed and turned by the consequences in everyone else's life. I hope his friendship with Tomas can give him some-thing solid to lean on, but I also feel protective of my son."

Nodding, Dirk studied her. "You know, I've been promising to take Caleb and Tomas pheasant hunting. Maybe I can get Hank's help, and we can take all four boys. It would be a fun break for Joey and Jack, too."

Emory reached up on her toes and kissed Dirk's cheek. She loved this tender side of him and knew he would be such a great dad if only he'd allow himself to be. A timer buzzed, and Dirk opened the oven. He peered inside and checked the theromometer. "Turkey's done!"

He pulled the large golden bird from the oven to rest while Emory and Teresa filled the serving dishes. Laurie called the boys and supervised their handwashing while everyone found their seats around the festive table. Creamy beeswax taper candles glowed, and colorful leaves strewn down the center made a beautiful runner.

After a delicious dinner filled with love, laughter, and friendly jibes, everyone rested in the living room waiting for their stomachs to gain enough room for pie. Ever the excellent host, Dirk made sure everyone had something to drink. He poured tumblers of crisp, amber twenty-year-old Macallan for Emory's father, Henry, and himself.

"Thank you, son." Her dad tapped his glass against Dirk's. "How about you join me for this drink out on the front porch? I'd like some fresh air, and I have a few things I want to discuss with you."

Dirk met Emory's gaze, and he winked. "Absolutely, Sir. Lead the way."

Emory's already stuffed gut felt ten pounds heavier as she watched the two most important men in her life walk through the door together.

30

Volodymyr sat in his leather chair facing the blazing fire above the hearth of the opulent living room in his New Jersey mansion. He puffed on his slender silver pipe as his men enjoyed Cuban cigars, filling the room with their scent. They were relaxing after stuffing themselves with roast turkey and all the traditional fixings. "You know, I truly enjoy the American tradition of Thanksgiving. I am honestly grateful to be an American citizen. The life that Burian Hordiyenko rescued me from was indeed nothing compared to the fortune I have here today. The opportunities in America are boundless." He raised his glass half filled with vodka. "Budmo!"

"Budmo!" The other men in the room lifted their glasses in response and repeated the Ukrainian cheer.

Staring into the fire, Volodymyr considered his next words with care. The others respectfully waited for him to speak. "While the women are clearing the dishes, we have business to discuss." An anxious quiet settled in the room. "Several days ago, after we received the phone call informing us that the US Marshals had placed the Bennington family into protective custody in Billings, Montana. I sent a team to grab Melissa Bennington. Will someone please tell me why I do not have the girl standing in this room before me, right now?"

Pavlo shifted his weight from foot to foot, and he drained his glass as all eyes turned to him. Volodymyr didn't want to hear his sniveling excuses. Pavlo's usefulness in the family was drawing to a rapid end. Beads of sweat popped out along the man's sparse hairline and dripped down his face. He mopped the moisture with a blue handkerchief. "We tried to grab her off the street when she was walking home from school, Vlod. But her brother showed up and fought Maksym off. We didn't want to cause a scene in the neighborhood and have the police called on us, so we drove away. By the time we went back to finish the job, there were cops parked all over outside watching the Benningtons' house. We have to wait till things cool down before we try again."

"Try?" Volodymyr slammed his glass down on the coffee table, splashing vodka out over his hand. "It's just the snatching of a little teenaged girl. How hard can it be? We do not have time for this! The trial gets closer every day and we need to shut her up. Permanently!" Volodymyr's heart raced with rage, and he puffed on his pipe to calm his anger. When he could once again control his voice, he asked, "What of the father?"

"We never made it that far."

Forcing his tone to remain steady, Volodymyr replied, "I'm aware. My ears are still blistered by the screaming phone call I received informing me of your incompetence. You must go back. We will keep that part of our deal." An evil glint lit his eyes. "But my priority is that girl! I want her in the basement of this house tonight! Dead or alive! As soon as you have her, kill them all. Do you understand me? There will be no more chances. If you do not have her here before sunup and can assure me you have annihilated the rest of her family, their ultimate fate will also become yours."

31

Joey's mom had never cooked Thanksgiving before. She had always had the holiday catered, and their household staff served them at their home in Connecticut. His mom complained about cooking all day. The gravy burned because the turkey wasn't done, and the green beans were cold. The meal was the worst Thanksgiving dinner Joey had ever had. It wasn't just that the Turkey was dry, and that the mashed potatoes were lumpy, but everyone at the table seemed angry at everyone else. Joey wasn't sure if he had anything to be grateful for.

After dinner, Joey helped his brother and sister clear the table and clean up the mess in the kitchen while their parents argued in the living room. The kids said nothing to each other as they worked. Joey brought dishes to the counter, Jack rinsed, and Kendall loaded the dishwasher. Silently, they listened to the hateful words spearing through the air in the other room.

Their mom cried, "How would you know? You're

never home! Where were you when that man grabbed Kendall?"

"I was at that useless job I'm forced to go to every day. Where do you think I was?"

"I don't know, but you weren't at your office when I tried to call you. Your daughter was almost kidnapped! She needed you!"

"Now you want me to account for every single minute of my day? Fine! For your information, I stopped to get a drink after work, if you must know." Their dad's words slammed against the walls. "I wish you could understand how impotent that pathetic job makes me feel. And don't tell me you don't miss the money I used to make, either. Because I know you do. And I can only imagine how Jack feels, losing his entire future career because of all this WITSEC bullshit!"

"It's better than being dead! That's the option, James. Maybe you need to get your mind wrapped around that! Besides, it isn't the job that makes you impotent."

"Oh, that's nice. Real nice. I understand we have no options, Ann. I'm not an idiot. But I don't have to like it!"

Her tone dropped, fear replacing her anger. "Do you think whoever tried to grab Kendall is from that Ukrainian mob family back in New Jersey?"

"I have no clue who they were." Joey's dad stopped shouting too. He sounded resigned and tired. "Not even the police know. Besides, how could they have found us?"

The boys finished putting the dishes in the dishwasher, while Kendall wiped down the counters. Joey's tummy hurt. He sniffed and swiped at tears on his cheeks. Kendall took his hand and led him to the kitchen table. She sat down and pulled him onto her lap.

"Hey, buddy, don't cry. Mom and Dad are just worried. That's why they're fighting."

Joey buried his face in her long brown hair. "I hate when they yell at each other."

Jack joined them and ruffled Joey's hair. "You gotta find a way to ignore them, bro. Let's go play video games in our room."

Joey's brother and sister tried to make him feel better, but they couldn't take away his fear. What was going to happen to them? Did the bad guys know where they lived now? Were his mom and dad going to get a divorce?

Their mother's voice rose from the other room, once again. "How would they find us? Gee, James, I don't know. Maybe by watching the movement on our hidden accounts that you shouldn't be messing with? Or more likely because you've been talking to Mindy. You're such an idiot, James. I can't believe you! You have put us all in jeopardy for that whore!"

Joey's stomach knotted hard, and he thought he might have to run to the toilet. "Mom knows about Mindy?" he asked his sister. A line formed between her eyebrows, and she shrugged.

Their dad yelled back. "It makes no sense to leave that money just sitting there! Why can't we use it here in this life? What if I want to buy a house that's bigger than this tin can? We could live like we used to. Don't you want that, Ann?"

"Sure. But that's not really your plan, is it? Your plan is to take all that money and run off with Mindy!" Their mother's voice elevated to shrill. "How could you choose her over me, James? Over us?"

There was a long silence before their father finally answered. "For one thing, she would never scream at me the way you do. She admires the work I do. She believes in me. You are always beating me down. No matter what I do, it's never good enough for you."

Joey's shoulders shook with silent sobs, and Kendall squeezed him closer. Jack slumped in the chair next to them, and rested his head against his crossed arms on the table.

"I see." His mother's tone had eerily calmed like the moments before a storm. "Well, the one thing I know, is if the Ukrainians have found us, it's all *your* fault."

32

The men slid on their jackets, topped off their drinks, and Dirk followed General Grey out the front door to the deep patio. He waited for Emory's father to take a seat. Dirk had been anticipating this discussion for weeks. He respected the fact that this man loved his daughter. But he didn't figure the general was going to be pleased to hear his thoughts on his and Emory's future together.

General Grey sat in one of four white rocking chairs padded with red cushions and indicated that Dirk should sit as well. He immediately took command of the discussion. "First, I'd like to thank you again for inviting us to your home for Thanksgiving dinner. It was a wonderful meal. Delicious turkey."

Bracing himself with his forearms on his knees, Dirk held his glass in both hands. "Thank you, Sir. It was an honor to have you."

"I'm going to cut through idle chitchat. We're both men. Both Marines. So, I'll put it out there straight.

Exactly what are your intentions regarding my daughter?"

Dirk kept his expression neutral, though he enjoyed an internal smirk. The man certainly didn't pull any punches. "I love Emory, Sir. I would like nothing more than to spend the rest of my life with her. However, we've discovered we have an insurmountable stumbling block."

The general's eyes narrowed slightly. "What on earth could that be? What obstacle is it you can't adapt to and overcome?"

"Your daughter dreams of having a family. I've already attempted that mission and failed. I don't wish to have any more children. Emory might agree to marry me anyway, but I refuse to ask her to make that sacrifice."

Emory's father studied him for several uncomfortable minutes, saying nothing. He took a large swallow of whiskey. Baring his teeth, he sucked in the cool early evening air, swallowed again, and cleared his throat. "I've read your jacket, and I know all about your history—the loss of your child and subsequent divorce. I think I understand where you're coming from. But I have some questions to ask you, and I want you to think about them. When you were active duty in Afghanistan, you fought shoulder to shoulder with your unit."

Dirk held the general's gaze and nodded. "Yes, Sir."

"Are you still friends with those men?"

"Of course. But I'd say those relationships go far beyond friendship."

"Yes. Your unit lost two men. Do you wish that you'd never met them?"

Dirk cocked his head and stared at the general. "Of

course not! They were some of the best men I've ever known. I'm a better man for knowing them and fighting beside them."

"Even though you've had to grieve their loss?"

The muscles in Dirk's stomach cinched tight. He realized where the general was going with this conversation. "Yes, but with all due respect, Sir, losing a child is different."

"More painful?"

It was Dirk's turn to swallow a gulp of liquid fortification. He waited to answer until he was sure his voice would remain steady. "Losing my son, Bennett, was the worst thing I've ever faced. I don't think I could survive something like that again."

"I am not belittling the incredible grief you must have gone through. I just want you to think about something." Dirk raised his eyes to the general. "If your friends, the men from your unit, needed you to fight with them again, would you do it?"

There was no doubt in Dirk's mind that if his friends needed him, he'd be on the next plane. But that was different, wasn't it? "Of course I would, Sir. But..."

"And how about young Hank in there?" The general waved his glass at the front door. "Any time you go out on a call, he could get killed. Yet, you remain his partner." The older man leaned toward Dirk until there was only a foot between their faces. "Listen to me. I have three daughters whom I love more than anything and for whom I would move heaven and earth. They have brought more joy into my life than any accomplishment or accolade that has come to me in my career. They also represent three terrifying possibilities for extreme grief. But I would never give up the joy they've given me in order to keep myself safe from losing them." The general paused and then softened his voice. "When you remember Bennett, how do you feel?"

Dirk coughed to clear the lump in his throat. "All these years later, my memories finally make me smile. He was a funny and sweet little guy. But I also feel a great sadness that I didn't get to see him grow up. Get to know him as a young man."

"Do you wish he was never born?"

Dirk glared at the general. A flash of anger so powerful coursed through him, that he nearly knocked the older man from his chair. But when the fury burned itself out, he realized the wisdom of what Emory's father was saying to him. "No. I'm grateful for every moment of his brief life."

"Well, then... I believe your intentions with Emory are honorable. You are both strong and capable adults, and I have no doubt you will figure everything out. And I want you to know that you're doing that with my blessing." The general stood and stuck out his hand.

Dirk rose to his feet, and blinking back stinging tears, he shook the general's hand. "Thank you, Sir. That means more than you know."

"Now let's go get some of that pie." Emory's father clapped him on the shoulder and guided him to the front door.

Emory stared at him when they came inside. He knew she was trying to read his emotions, but he held a poker face. Giving up on him, her gaze swung to her father, who winked at her and asked when they were having dessert.

Hank broke the tension. "Come on, T. Let's dish up some of that pie. Did you bring the pecan? Because that's my favorite."

Emory joined them and brought Dirk a slice of pumpkin pie loaded with whipped cream. He stuffed an enormous bite into his mouth, but before he could swallow, his phone beeped with a text. He glanced at the words and his blood ran cold.

Kendall: HELP! They're here! They found us! HELP!

Dirk jumped to his feet, the pie plate clattering to the floor.

Emory rushed to his side. "What is it? What's wrong?"

Dirk showed her the text. "Hank. Grab your go bag. We've got to go!"

Without questioning him, Hank ran to the guest room to get what he needed. Emory called 911 and was speaking to the dispatcher while Dirk darted to the hall closet to grab his gear. Teresa went to Emory's side. "What do you need from me, Chief?"

"Stay here and man the phones. Laurie, would you mind taking my parents back to my apartment?"

General Grey stood tall. "Emory, you and your team do what you need to do. We will manage everything else. Don't give it any thought."

"Thanks, Dad. I'll see you both later." Emory followed Dirk. "I'm coming with you. My gear is in my car. SWAT will meet us there." She dashed out the door to grab her body armor and firearms. Hank was on her heels.

Dirk checked the magazine in his gun and automatically ran his fingers over the spare ammunition clipped to his utility belt. The general gripped his arm, and Dirk paused to meet his eye. "Keep her safe."

"You know I will," Dirk assured him. Before he dashed out the door, he made eye contact with Teresa and Laurie. "It's going to be a long night. We'll stay in touch." With that, Dirk ran out into the night.

33

After they cleaned up the mess from dinner and things had settled down with her parents, Kendall took refuge in her room. Her brothers had done the same in their shared bedroom, zoning out with video games. She watched the Charlie Brown Christmas Special on her iPad while scrolling through her old friends' social media accounts on her phone. She knew she wasn't supposed to, but it couldn't hurt anything if she just looked. It stung that their high school had lost five students, including her, and yet their friends all just moved on with life as if nothing had happened. Sure, there were the funerals, and kids posted memories for a while, but then life went back to normal... without them.

Kendall longed for someone she could share her thoughts and feelings with, but she had no one. She decided to write everything out in her new journal. "Dear Diary, Fletcher and Delaney are obviously still an item. Delaney is one of a handful of junior varsity cheerleaders the team brought up to the varsity cheer squad after the tragedy. It seems she and Fletcher are the new sophomore class "It Couple". I know I'm obsessing over my past life, and it's super depressing, but I can't seem to stop. I haven't made any new friends in Billings, so what else am I supposed to do?

"Jack already has a group of guys he hangs out with. Being an athlete makes it so easy for him. Besides, boys aren't as cliquey as girls. Even Joey has a new best bud." She tapped her pen that had a fuzzy pink pompom glued to its end against the lined paper. "I guess I have to admit that I haven't really *tried* to make any new friends. It's hard to look forward when I want to move backwards. I want to go home, but that will never happen."

Switching from her old friends' feeds, she signed in to Insta on her new Kendall Miller profile and searched for posts from her current high school. It was too late to try out for cheer this year, but she could join a club. Maybe Yearbook, or the school newspaper. Either of those options would help her get involved and meet people.

Like a new bud in spring, hope slowly unfurled its first tender petals. As difficult as it was for Kendall to move on. It was time. With fresh energy, she navigated to the high school website and clicked on the drop-down menu for clubs. But before she dug in, she decided to celebrate her new direction with a piece of pumpkin pie.

On her way to the kitchen, Kendall noticed her mother had closed herself in her parents' bedroom, and her dad was reading in the front room. That explained the stillness in the house. Kendall stuck her head into her brother's room. "Hey, guys?" They didn't answer because their headphones were on. She threw a shoe at them and got their attention.

Jack unplugged the headsets, and the game music blared from the TV. "What?"

"Do you guys want some pie? I'm getting a piece."

Joey perked up. "Yeah! I do! With lots of Cool Whip!"

She laughed. "I'm sure there's plenty. Come on."

Without looking away from their game, Jack said, "Bring me a piece too, will ya?"

"I guess, but it'll cost you." Kendall waited for Joey to climb off his bed and join her.

Jack glanced at her. "What's your price?"

"You have to let me sit with you and your friends at lunch on Monday."

Space battle sounds increased as Jack's thumbs flew around his controller. "Why?"

"Because. Is it a deal?"

"I guess." He shrugged. "Tanner Dunn thinks you're cute. But he's just a freshman like me."

"He does?" A kernel of happiness glowed inside her heart. Jack smirked and plugged his headset back in. Yep. She knew without question that it was *finally* time to move on.

She and Joey brought three plates of pie from the kitchen. After dropping Jack's dessert off on his nightstand, Kendall returned to her room to read more about the Yearbook Club. But before she did, she looked up Tanner's profile on Instagram. He was pretty cute, with his long sandy-blond bangs. Baseball appeared to be his major interest, and Kendall's heart ached for Jack. Nothing about their new life was fair to him.

Kendall had filled her mouth with a huge dollop of whipped cream when she heard a loud crash. Someone was yelling in the living room. Her parents were at it again. She rolled her eyes and pulled her noise cancelling headphones over her ears and scrolled down through Tanner's posts.

She glimpsed her mom through the open crack in her door, storming down the hallway toward the living room. Pressing the volume, she turned it up to tune out her parent's next blow up when another movement caught her eye. Kendall pulled one ear pad away from her head to hear if one of her brothers was talking to her. She heard only muffled sounds, so she replaced her headphones.

A sound so loud it shook the walls caused her to sit up. She yanked the headset off, quickly realizing the voices she heard yelling were not those of her parents. The words were deep and commanding—a mixture of accented English and a language she didn't understand.

A scream rose in her throat as terror washed through her. She clapped a hand over her mouth to keep the sound inside. The Ukrainians had found them! They were in their house! Her trembling thumbs flew across her phone screen. She texted the one man she hoped could save them.

"HELP! They're here! They found us! HELP!"

34

With her heart echoing like a bass drum, Kendall peered through the crack between her door and the wall. She was breathing so hard, she thought she might pass out. She did her best to slow down her panting. A tall gunman dressed in black, and built like a tree trunk made his way down the hall, his heavy boots thudding against the floor. Kendall clapped a hand over her mouth to trap the scream searing its way up her throat. The intruder opened the bathroom door, and finding no one inside, he slammed it shut.

Next, he threw open the entrance to her brothers' room. He yelled at Jack and Joey with unintelligible words, but the waving of his weapon made his demands clear. Jack wrapped his arm protectively around Joey and he pushed their little brother behind him.

The hulk growled. "Come. Now. Or I kill you where you stand." He reached for them, grabbing Jack's arm. Jack slapped the muzzle of the man's gun out of his face and jerked away from his grip. The Ukrainian shoved Jack in the chest. Reacting, Jack pushed back with both hands, earning a sharp crack from the man's pistol grip on the side of his head. Blood erupted from Jack's hairline above his temple, and he collapsed, unconscious, to the floor. Joey wailed in fear, and the thug grabbed a handful of his shirt and tossed him down the hall toward the front room.

Terror seized Kendall's body, and she cried out before she could stop herself, giving away her location. Her heart slammed against its rib-lined cage. A plan for escape flashed through her mind. She darted for the window, yanking it open in hope of escaping into the back yard. Kendall threw her leg over the sill, ducking through the narrow opening. Her bare toes felt dirt beneath them, but her pursuer was too fast. He grabbed hold the ankle still inside and pulled her back into the room. Kendall dug her fingernails into the trim, and kicked at him, but she was no match against the man's strength.

"Here you are! Our prize. Where did you think you were going?" She cowered on the floor at his feet. Laughing, the brute knotted his fist in her hair and pulled her across the floor behind him. In one long stride, he flung open her door. The knob bashed through the drywall behind it and stuck. He yanked Kendall to her feet. His powerful fingers dug painfully into her arm like a vice as he rushed her past her unconscious brother toward the living room. Desperately, Kendall dug her heels into the carpeted floor, but it was no use.

"Jack!" Kendall screamed as she clawed at the man's

fingers. "Let go of me!" She grabbed at the doorframe of the bathroom leaving scratch marks in the wood.

The man stumbled which angered him. "Stop fighting me, little *sraka!*" He smashed Kendall's head against the wall for punishment. Her vision dimmed as pain radiated through her skull.

The man easily overpowered her and half lifting her off her feet, he propelled her down the hall. He shoved her hard and she spilled onto the living room floor joining Joey and their parents huddled together in front of the sofa. He pointed the sinister black pistol at them.

The scene from Esme's slumber party super-imposed itself on Kendall's current reality. She gagged on the horrific memories. Joey buried his face in her shoulder, but utter terror prevented her from comforting him. Yet, instinctively, her body curled around his in futile protection.

There were two men, just like before. Images of her friend's deaths flashed through her mind like slides, paralyzing her with fear. Those murderers had fired on the innocent girls without hesitation, and Kendall realized there was nothing she could do now to save herself or her family.

Her dad crawled to the front of their huddle, pushing his family behind him. Everyone in the family, including him, was in tears. He raised up on his knees and held open, surrendering palms to the intruders. "Please! Please don't hurt us. I have money. Lots of money. I will pay you to let us go. I'll pay you more than you're making to kill us." He clasped his fingers together before his chest, pleading.

Of the two attackers, the one who seemed in charge displayed decaying teeth when he grinned, and in a thick Slavic accent said, "Oh, don't worry, Mr. Miller. Or more accurately, Mr. Bennington. We already have plenty of your money. Thanks to your loving wife." The man sneered at Kendall's mother. He raised his gun, aimed it at her father, and fired. He glared at Kendall's mom. "Consider our account closed."

The exploding shot pierced Kendall's eardrums, and her heart stopped. Her ears rang. Her throat stung with spent gunpowder. Screaming, she sprang toward her father's fallen body. "No! No! Daddy! No!" She glared up at the gunman through a veil of tears. "How could you? Why? He's not the one you want! It's me! *I'm* the one who saw you killing my friends!" Sobbing, she wrapped her arms around her dad's limp form. Hot blood flowed through her fingers as she tried desperately to hold what remained of the back of her father's skull together.

"Yes, of course, *Myla*. You are the reason we're here. Volodymyr Kovalenko has requested your presence at his home. If you behave, you will live long enough to make his acquaintance. If you do not, you will follow the fate of your *Tato*. Come!" His comrade grabbed Kendall by her arm and yanked her to her feet. Her father's blood dripped to the carpet from her fingers.

Her mother held Joey's face against her breast to shield him from the scene, but when the man pulled Kendall away, she pushed Joey aside. Screaming she lunged toward her daughter, trying to tug her away from her captor. "No! You can't do this! We had a deal! You promised!"

The man in charge laughed a phlegm-filled chortle as he gripped a handful of her mother's hair and forced her to her knees before him. "You dare to bargain with Kovalenko? Ha! He owns you!" He back handed her across the face. Blood spurted from her nose as he tossed her aside. "Besides, we took care of our side of the deal. And now I must follow Kovalenko's orders." His voice rose and fell in a sing-songy tone. "Alas, we cannot leave the three of you behind when we take your daughter." He aimed his weapon at her mother's bloody face. And Kendall knew the true taste of horror.

She screamed and fought to get away from her captor. Suddenly, Jack lunged out of the hallway holding a bedside lamp above his head. He threw it at the man threatening their mother. It hit the Ukrainian's head, temporarily stunning him. Jack took the opportunity and dove at him, wrapping his arms around the shooter's knees, he tackled him to the floor. A muzzle flash blinded Kendall's eyes in the evening's dusk as the man's gun flew from his hand. The report assaulted her already damaged ears.

"Jack!" she screamed. Bits of fabric and fluff puffed from the hole in the couch where the stray bullet seared into its cushion. Relief flowed over her like iced water.

The front door crashed open.

Glass exploded into crumbles of safety glass as the sliding door in the kitchen disintegrated. SWAT officers poured in through the doors.

Jack wrestled with the man underneath him, unable to triumph over his size and brute strength. The large man rolled away grasped his loose gun and snatched

Joey. Kneeling, he held the little boy before him as a human shield. "Get out! Or I'll snap this kid's neck like a twig!"

Kendal battled with all her might, helpless to escape the clutches of the man who held her. Jack hurled himself at the man gripping Joey, managing to knock his gun hand away from their brother. A second shot went off. One of the officers dropped to the floor.

In the chaos, the man holding Kendall reached into his jacket and pulled out black corrugated oval device. He bit down on a ring attached to the top and pulled. Swinging his arm over his head, he launched the dark object into the kitchen.

"Grenade!" One of the cops yelled. A great flash and bang exploded in the night, stunning everyone inside the house. Kendall bit down hard on her captor's wrist and he screamed but tightened his grip on her.

More black-clad, helmeted figures carrying black rifles poured into the house in a steady coordinated fashion, shouting, "Police! Drop Your Weapons! Drop them now!"

The man restraining Kendall clamped his injured arm tightly around her throat, cutting off her air. He pressed his gun to her temple. "Don't come any closer, or I will kill her!"

Through a haze of burning tears, Kendall struggled to make sense of what was happening.

Then she saw him. Deputy Sterling. He and his partner had joined the police team and entered their home. He swung his pistol, aiming it directly at her captor's face. "Let her go! There's no way out of this for you." His gaze shifted slightly, and his eyes bored into hers, sharing his courage.

"That's where you're wrong! She is my way out. Lay down your weapons and allow me to leave, or I will blow her head off where she stands!" The man's hot breath filled her ear and moistened her neck. Kendall's stomach clenched and bile rose in her throat.

Deputy Sterling's onyx eyes glinted behind his clear visor. "If you shoot her, I'll kill you. Let her go, and you'll live."

"I don't believe you! Besides, if I let her go, Kovalenko will kill me anyway." The man's hand twitched on his gun, and he squeezed the trigger. His hand jerked as he pulled the metal lever.

Click.

Nothing!

His gun misfired! Kendall's knees buckled, but the man held her against him. He pressed the muzzle firmer into her skull.

Another shot rang out. The sound pierced Kendall's eardrums. The man holding her screamed and loosened his grip as his shoulder burst into a firework of blood, tissue, and bone. He was forced to turn with the power of the blast and a second shot hit him right between the eyes.

Kendall and her would-be killer dropped toward the floor.

Before she hit the ground, Deputy Sterling had her in his arms.

"You're okay, Kendall. I've got you." His deep voice murmured in her hair as he held her tightly against his solid form and wiped the dead man's splattered blood from her face.

Deputy Flannigan skidded to his knees at their side. "Nice shot, Sterling," he said as he pivoted with his weapon, prepared to cover them.

Within seconds, police pulled Joey from the other Ukrainian's grip and made the killer lie face down on the floor. More officers checked and cleared the remainder of the house. Someone rushed to her mother who sat in stunned silence against the couch. Jack crawled toward Joey who had curled up in the corner of the room crying. The little guy lifted his thumb to his mouth when Jack wrapped his arms around his thin shoulders. A cop checked her father's body. He made eye contact with Sterling and shook his head.

Kendall convulsed with wracking sobs. Sterling held her, supporting her body while she fell apart. Sudden fury erupted in her soul, and she pounded her fists against his chest. "Where were you? Why didn't you get here faster?" she screamed in rage and anguish.

"It's okay. I've got you. You're safe now." Sterling kept his strong arms around her while she dissolved.

A beautiful blonde woman approached them and stroked Kendall's long hair out of her face, draping it behind her ear. "Kendall? My name is Emory. You're safe now, sweetheart. You and your brothers are incredibly brave."

Kendall blinked at the woman. A sudden spear of panic ran through her heart. "My brothers! Where are they?" she cried.

The woman motioned to a police officer who brought

her youngest brother over to her. "Jack is in the kitchen getting medical attention for a cut on his head. But it sounds like he's going to be just fine. You are all safe now."

Kendall numbly scanned the space. Blood and broken glass seemed to cover every surface. EMTs attended to Jack's head and her father's body. She met her mother's eyes from across the room. Confusion and pure hatred such as she'd never felt seared through her brain and the bile that had been simmering in her gut rose in her throat like a tidal wave. Kendall tried to turn away before her stomach emptied itself in rebellion, but the retching came before she could. Deputy Sterling didn't flinch or turn away. He simply held her fast, rubbing her back as her body rejected the night's events. "That's it. Let it out. I've got you."

He knelt, holding her for what seemed like hours, as police officers came and went. First responders checked over her surviving family members. They zipped her father's body in a black bag that matched the one they had placed the dead Ukrainian in, and took him away, and the weight of the night crashed over her.

Finally, when Kendall's mind began to clear, and she noticed her brothers sat with Deputy Flannigan, who held Joey on his knee as he spoke quietly with Jack.

The nice blonde woman returned with a warm washcloth for Kendall and a hand towel for Deputy Sterling. "Dirk, CPS is here. They want to escort the children to the hospital, where a doctor is waiting to examine them."

Kendall's body trembled uncontrollably, and Deputy Sterling called for someone to bring him a blanket. "She's going into shock." He wrapped the blanket around her and lifted her in his arms.

Kendall met his gaze. "Who is CPS?"

Sterling clenched his teeth, and the muscles rippled in his jaw. "Child Protective Services. They're here to make sure that you and your brothers are safe and cared for. But first, you need to see a doctor."

"Will you come with us?"

"Try and stop me."

35

Dirk refused to let the Miller kids out of his sight, and he rode with them in the ambulance to the hospital. He had tossed his coat with US MARSHALS emblazoned on the back into a plastic bag and replaced it with his leather jacket. His jeans were still a mess, but thanks to the rag Emory brought him, they would do until he could change.

Emory and Hank followed them to the emergency room in Dirk's car. When they got there, the ER was chaotic with police guarding their prisoner and the marshals watching over the children. Physician's assistants and nurses scrambled to keep up with the mayhem.

Thankfully, the hospital staff allowed the Miller kids to stay together in one exam room while they waited for the doctor to come. Dirk and Hank remained with them while Emory spoke with a representative from Child Protective Services in the lobby.

"Deputy Sterling?" Kendall looked up at him with haunted eyes.

"Call me Dirk."

A ghost of a smile passed across her lips. "Dirk. What's going to happen to us? What's going to happen to my mother?"

He hesitated to answer. How could he add more agony to these broken children than they were already carrying? But knowing they needed an answer, he cleared his throat. "My boss, Emory Grey, the woman you met earlier, is trying to sort that out right now. Please don't worry." Dirk said the words as much to himself as to Kendall. The last thing he wanted was for these kids to get dumped into the system. They deserved better than that. "She's with the police."

"Did they arrest her?"

Dirk worked his jaw and nodded. He hated like hell to have to tell her. "Yeah."

"What for, exactly?" Her voice wobbled.

He looked into her eyes for a long minute before answering. "For conspiracy to commit murder. She's being interviewed by detectives at the police department, right now."

Kendall's dark eyes widened. "Does that mean *she* hired those men to kill my dad?"

"That's what we think." The girl's grief tore at his heart. "I'm sorry."

A nurse entered the room and smiled at everyone. "I'm Mary, And I'm here to make sure you have everything you need. Which one of you boys is Jack?"

Jack, who sat on the bed in the center of the small room, raised his hand a scant inch off the mattress.

"Well, that makes sense." Mary's smile broadened.

"Since you're the one with the bandaged head. I'm going to clean your wound and get everything ready for the doctor's examination. Will that be alright?"

The boy shrugged a shoulder. He hadn't said a word all night. These kids had been through hell, and Dirk was determined to keep them from dealing with any more trauma. The nurse explained each of her actions as she went along, occasionally resting her hand on Jack's shoulder to comfort him. Yet still, he remained silent.

Dirk was least concerned about Joey because, though they'd all been traumatized by the night's events, Joey had cried it out and seemed able to talk about what happened while Kendall seemed fragile and remained in shock. And Jack... his injuries ran far deeper than the abrasion on his head. Not only had the kids been terrified for their lives, but they'd witnessed their father's brutal murder, and their mother had betrayed them all. How would they ever overcome that?

The ER doctor tapped on the door and entered the room, followed by Emory. "I'm Doctor Silva and it's my job to check you kids out and make sure you're all right. We'll start here with Jack." The man crossed the room, pulled a penlight from a pocket in his lab coat, and aimed it at the laceration on Jack's head. "Boy, I bet that didn't feel good." He parted Jack's hair in different sections and then addressed the nurse. "I'd like to give Jack here a couple of stitches. Please prep the wound." He turned to Dirk and Emory. "It's likely that Jack has a concussion. I will send information on concussion protocols with him when he leaves here. Will you make certain they're followed?" He moved on to examine the other two kids.

Dirk glanced at Emory, who nodded. How could they be sure that someone they didn't know would follow the doctor's orders? Biting on his lower lip, he crossed his arms over his chest.

Doctor Silva knelt before Joey and chatted with him for a few minutes. After determining that the boy was at least physically fine, he stood and turned toward Kendall. "I'd like you to step into the room next door so that I can examine you privately."

Kendall shot a terrified glance at Dirk and that was all it took. "No. She goes nowhere without me."

The doctor smiled condescendingly. "Sir, you may stand right outside the door. But it would be inappropriate for you to be inside the exam room with us. I'll have nurse Mary with me. Will that be alright?"

Dirk was about to protest when Emory placed her hand on his arm to quiet him. "That's fine, Doctor. Kendall, Dirk and I will be right outside if you need anything. Unless you'd like me to come in the exam room with you?"

"No, thanks." The poor girl was terrified. "I'll be alright." She looked at Dirk with questioning eyes.

He bobbed his head, hoping to reassure her. Reaching forward, he cupped her cold cheek. "I promise I'll only be a few feet away."

Dirk and Emory followed as the nurse guided Kendall to the exam room next door. He motioned for Hank to stay with the boys. When the door closed behind Kendall, Dirk positioned himself in front of it, planting his feet apart and crossing his arms over his chest like a bouncer at a club.

"There is no need to worry, Dirk. The children are safe here." Emory ran her hands up and down his arms as though to warm him.

"I don't want them to just *be* safe. I want them to *feel* safe."

"I doubt they will feel that way for a long while. When they're done here, CPS is waiting to take them to temporary housing until they can place them. I have the feeling their mother's going away for a long time."

Dirk swallowed against his thickening throat. "Will they keep the kids together in foster care?" His chest was heavy, crushing his heart and making breathing difficult.

Emory looked him in the eye but took her time answering. Finally, she said, "No. I doubt they'll be able to keep them together. It's rare that foster families have that much extra room."

"This is wrong, Em. I don't like it. There's got to be another way."

She leaned into him, slid her arms around his waist, and pressed her cheek against his chest, but said nothing.

36

Emory and Dirk stayed with the children until they had all seen the doctor. She sent Hank to follow up with the police department and ask that they keep them informed about the situation with Ann Miller. CPS agents waited in the lobby to take custody of the kids, but Dirk refused to let them out of his sight.

He positioned himself between the agents and the children. "I can't allow you to have custody of these kids. This family is in the Federal Witness Protection Program, which makes them *my* responsibility. We cannot expect either temporary or permanent placement parents to accept them without knowing the danger they would put themselves in."

It amazed Emory as each of the Miller kids moved toward Dirk, as though magnetically drawn to him. It was obvious they felt safe with him. A smile swept over her lips. She knew the feeling.

"I'm sorry, Deputy Sterling. I realize this is an unusual

situation, but it is our job to protect children and provide them with a safe home. But what alternative do you have?"

"They can stay at my house."

"That's not possible."

A hot coal burned behind Dirk's sternum. "Why the hell not? I can't think of a safer place for them right now."

"You have never gone through the process of determining whether your home is appropriate and safe for children. I cannot allow you to take these kids somewhere that hasn't been pre-approved by our agency."

Even from across the room, Emory could feel the tension building inside the man she loved. The features on his face seemed to sharpen along with his glare. "Fine. What do we need to do to gain approval to provide temporary placement of them?"

The agent stammered and glanced at her partner. "Well, the process usually takes several weeks, if not months."

"These kids are not going anywhere with you. It's not safe. Their lives are in danger, and because of that, yours would be too. I suggest you expedite your process. We can go to my house right now, and you can do what you need to do to grant us approval to care for them for the time being."

Emory's jaw dropped open. She was astounded at what she was hearing. Did Dirk truly intend to be the temporary foster placement for the Miller kids? Clearly, he hadn't thought this through.

The CPS agent looked at each of the children in turn, then addressed Kendall. "Is this what you want?"

Again, the kids moved closer to Dirk, and all three said, "Yes," nodding vehemently.

"OK, I need to call my supervisor." She smiled up at Dirk. "At least we know you'll pass the background check. I suppose we can come to your house right now for a preliminary check. If my supervisor agrees, the kids will have a safe place to spend the night. Chief Grey, I assume you will spend the night at Deputy Sterling's house as well? We won't gain approval for Kendall to stay with him without an adult female present."

Startled, Emory met Dirk's gaze. The intensity of the question in his eyes wrung her heart. "Of course." She stepped toward the CPS agent. "That makes the most sense. After all, the safety of these children is the responsibility of the US Marshals Office. But it's more than that." She faced Dirk. "We want them to be with us."

The approval that shone in Dirk's eyes filled her heart with joy. Could this really be happening? Was Dirk demanding to take on not one, but three children? To protect and care for them for an indeterminate amount of time?

The agent wrote a few notes in her handheld notebook and then beamed at them. "Given the circumstance, I think this is the best solution, too. And it certainly makes our job easier. Few people are willing to foster three older kids at once. Especially when there's danger involved. Thank you. I'll let you know as soon as I hear from my boss."

Dirk jotted down his address for the agent before he and Emory moved the kids to a private waiting room where they would be more comfortable. Kendall, Jack, and Joey sat huddled together on the small couch, and within minutes, Joey was asleep on Kendall's lap. Emory and Dirk sat in chairs opposite them.

Kendall spoke quietly so as not to wake her brother. "Deputy Sterling?" She blinked. "What's gonna happen to my mom?"

"First of all, since you're going to be staying with us for a while, remember you can call me Dirk. And this is Emory. I haven't heard from Deputy Flannigan—whose name is Hank, by the way—but I know she'll be spending time in the local jail until a judge sets bail, which may or may not happen. Then she'll need to stand trial for what happened tonight."

Tears flashed in Jack's eyes, and his cheeks grew blotchy with the effort of restraining them. He spoke for the first time that night. "I can't believe she made a deal with those guys to kill our dad! I can't believe that happened!" The boy jumped to his feet, jammed his hands in his jeans pockets and hurried to the window, turning his back on them.

Dirk followed him and rested a reassuring hand on the boy's shoulder. At his touch, Jack turned his face into Dirk's chest and his body jerked with bitter sobs. Dirk wrapped strong arms around the devastated youth and held him until his tears subsided. The sight of them together like that moved Emory deeply. Her heart shifted inside. This was a layer of the man she loved that she had never seen before. Kendall wept softly and Emory reached for her hand. There were no words that would comfort these children. All she and Dirk could do was provide a safe place, and care for them while they grieved.

The CPS agent poked her head around the corner into the room. "I just received approval for you to take the kids home with you tonight. We'll send a team over in the morning to expedite the approval process for temporary placement."

Keeping his arm around the boy's shoulders as they walked, Dirk returned to the group with Jack. "Good. Come on, Emory. Let's get these kids home." He reached down and lifted the sleeping Joey in his arms and led the way out to his Jeep.

They drove in silence to the outskirts of Billings, where Dirk's farmhouse was located. When they got there, they found that Teresa and Laurie had cleaned up the Thanksgiving dinner. They had also packed Hank's belongings for him and cleared out from the bedroom he'd been using. His things were stacked neatly by the front door.

Emory smoothed her hand across the bedspread. "Looks like the ladies put fresh sheets on the bed, too. Everything is ready for the kids." She smiled up at Dirk.

Dirk slipped Joey's shoes off, and after pulling back the covers, he laid the boy on the bed. "Jack, for tonight, you and Joey will need to share this bed. Kendall, the room next door is for you. I realize you don't have any of your things. We can take care of that tomorrow, but for tonight, you can borrow a couple of T-shirts from me to sleep in. For now, I want you to rest assured that you are safe, and that Emory and I are going to be with you every step of the way as we sort everything out."

Kendall flung her arms around his neck and buried her face in his chest. "I don't know what we would do without you, Dirk. Thank you so much. I'm so sorry to put you through all this."

Dirk drew back and lifted her chin. He looked into her eyes. "None of this is your fault, Kendall. And we're happy that you're here with us. Okay?" She nodded, and he hugged her tightly. "Are either of you hungry? I know there's some pie around here somewhere. Emory?"

At the mention of her name, Emory snapped out of a sort of trance she had fallen into as she watched Dirk take the lead in caring for the children. "Yes, of course. There are also plenty of leftovers if you'd rather have more of a meal." She hurried to the kitchen, glad to have something tangible to do.

By two in the morning, the kids were all finally asleep, and Emory joined Dirk in his bed. "I never would have guessed when I got up this morning that I'd end the day with three kids in the house and in bed with you." Emory snuggled against him. "It's been a hell of a day. I still want to know what my dad said to you this afternoon, but I'm too tired to listen."

Dirk held her close. His voice sagged with exhaustion. "Your dad said all the things a good dad should say. Rest easy. We have a big day ahead of us tomorrow." His words trailed off as he drifted into sleep.

37

The following morning brought with it the stark reality of the situation the Miller kids found themselves in. Their father was dead, and their mother was in jail for his murder. They had effectively been abandoned.

Emory had woken before anyone and rummaged through Dirk's refrigerator for breakfast food. She started a pot of coffee and cooked a pound of bacon. Kendall was the next to rise, and she stumbled sleepily out of her room. Emory smiled at the girl, wanting to encourage her. "Do you drink coffee, or would you prefer milk or orange juice?"

"You would let me drink a cup of coffee? Do you have cream and sugar?" Kendall slid onto a bar stool at the kitchen island.

"I think after all you've been through, you can have a cup of coffee. Don't you?" Emory filled a mug and set it in front of Kendall before bringing her the sugar bowl and a carton of cream. "How are you feeling this morning?"

The girl shrugged but didn't answer, and her shoulders curled forward self-protectively. Emory made a note to ask the CPS agent about getting all the kids into therapy. "You know, Kendall, you are an amazingly strong young woman. You've been through hell, and you're still standing. I'm really proud of you."

"We both are." Dirk emerged from the master bedroom wearing plaid-flannel sleep pants and a T-shirt. His black hair poked out at odd angles, and he had never looked more attractive to Emory than at that moment. She poured him a cup of coffee and kissed him as she passed him the mug. "What do you guys want for breakfast?"

"Pancakes!" Shouted Joey from his bedroom door. He skipped out in front of Jack, who followed him with plodding steps. But as Joey gauged his sister's somber expression, his mood dampened. He curled into the corner of the couch and Emory wondered if memories from the night before had conquered his morning innocence.

Emory made the requested pancakes which the kids ate in solemn silence. She made several attempts at lightening the mood with talk of the beautiful weather and the nice view, but the children did not engage. After breakfast, Emory cleaned up the dishes while the children took turns in the shower.

At nine o'clock sharp, two CPS agents knocked on the front door.

THE TWO WOMEN spent over an hour inspecting Dirk's home. They talked with each of the kids separately, then called a meeting with everyone. Dirk and Emory joined the children in the living room to face the agents.

"Good news," said the shorter, plump woman with silver hair. "Your house passes the inspection with flying colors. Except, of course, you will need to replace the queen size bed in the boy's room with two individual beds."

"Not a problem. We can do that today." Dirk nodded at the boys.

"Perfect. I saw the gun safe in your bedroom. That must remain locked at all times." She turned to address the children. "Now, we should have permanent placement for each of you kids in a couple of weeks. Unfortunately, we'll have to separate you, but you will be allowed to see each other on weekends."

Kendall gasped, and Dirk rose to his feet. "Absolutely not. This family has gone through too much to have to deal with being separated on top of it. Besides, I don't have the confidence in regular foster parents to provide the type of protective environment these kids need."

The agent responded calmly. "I understand your concern, Deputy Sterling. This is an unusual and terrible situation. Unfortunately, however, it's likely the best that we can do."

"Well, it's not the best *I* can do. The children will stay here with me." He turned and looked deeply into Emory's eyes. "With us." He said it as a statement, but really it was a question. Would Emory agree to take on such a commitment with him? He doubted he could do a good job on his own, though he was willing to try if she didn't agree. These poor kids didn't deserve the life they found themselves in. Someone needed to step up and take care of them, and that meant keeping them together and making sure they were safe.

Emory stared at him. He could see hundreds of questions swimming in her eyes. Questions he didn't have answers for, at least not right then. He waited.

Gradually, her head moved up and down. "Yes, Dirk. You and the children can count on me."

Two knocks sounded against the front door before it swung open, and an exhausted Hank walked in. "Good morning." He took in the scene in the living room. "Am I interrupting something?"

Dirk introduced him to the CPS agents and explained the purpose of their meeting. "Emory's willing to help me take care of the kids. But it looks like you've lost your room."

"I figured as much when Teresa called me last night."

"Have you been at the PD all night?"

"Yeah." Hank passed a furtive glance at the kids and dropped his voice. "It's not looking good for Mrs. Miller."

Emory stood, slid her hand around Dirk's elbow, and returned to the subject of housing. "Hank, since I'll be staying here at Dirk's, maybe you could sublease my apartment. If you'd like."

Hank rubbed his chin. "That actually solves a problem for me. I was planning on finding a more permanent place of my own, anyway. Thanks. That would at least buy me some time."

"Takes care of two problems at once, then." She

smiled softly. "My parents are currently staying in the guest room at my apartment, but they're leaving tomorrow."

Hank shrugged and slumped into one of the living room chairs. "No problem, as long as they don't mind me crashing there tonight."

"I'll call them and explain the turn of events. I'm sure they won't mind, at all."

The CPS agents agreed to take Dirk's request to their supervisor, and they left the newly formed family to settle in.

Hank pulled Dirk aside. "Ann Miller has confessed that she had arranged and paid for the murder of her husband. She believed she had made a solid deal with Kovalenko. She had given him what he told her was enough money for him to kill James, and to leave Kendall alone. Not surprisingly, the mob boss lied. He sent his men to murder James Miller and then kill Kendall and the rest of the family."

"Thank God we got there in time. It's awful what happened to James. He was an ass, but he didn't deserve to die. And it makes me sick the kids had to see him get shot."

"It will be hard for them to overcome it." Hank glanced over to where the siblings were huddled together on the couch. "Eventually, the kids can visit their mother, if they want to."

"I'll let them know."

"As far as the Ukrainian thug, he's singing away hoping to cut a deal with the DA. Seems he'd rather roll on his boss than face the death penalty."

"That's good news. Do they realize that they'll still probably spend the rest of their lives in prison?"

Hank held his arms akimbo. "That's up to a judge to decide."

"Listen, kid." Dirk shoved his fingers through his hair. He had something important to do, the thought of which made him queasy. "Will you do me a favor and sit with the kids for a little while? I need to talk to Emory."

"Sure. I want to help with them as much as I can. I'm pretty much always available for babysitting or whatever."

"Thanks." Dirk went in search of Emory and found her reading a story to Joey from her phone.

"We have no children's books, so I got one on my Kindle app." She grinned up at him.

"We have a lot of things we need, and a lot to take care of. In fact, I need to speak with you for a minute. Will you go on a walk with me?" He picked Joey up off the bed. "Hank's in the living room. You want to hang out with him for a little bit?"

"Yeah!" Joey wriggled out of his grasp and ran into the main room. Dirk held his hand out to Emory.

They walked along Dirk's property line as he pointed out the spots where he wanted to build a barn and start a vegetable garden. "I think I could add on to the back of the house. I'm on twenty acres here. Plenty of space for kids, don't you think? And of course, I have the cabin up in the mountains, too. I make less than you, but it's still a pretty good living."

Emory stopped walking and looked at him with confusion. "What are you getting at, Sterling?"

He faced her and was in that moment overwhelmed by his feelings for her. Taking her hands in his, he dropped to his knees in the dirt before her. "Emory Sue Grey, you know I love you. I love you more than life itself. You've put up with a lot more from me than you should have, and still, you stand by me. I promise I'll do my damnedest to live up to your dedication, if you will do me the honor of becoming my wife."

She reached for his face and searched his eyes. "What about children? We never settled that issue."

"I guess I'm going to have to overcome my fear. After all, we already have three kids in the house right now who need us, and after that, what's a few more?"

EPILOGUE

Dirk sat hip and elbow next to Hank in economy seating on a commercial flight with his knees bumping the back of the chair in front of him. A woman sat to his left in the window seat, and he did his best not to crowd her. He and Hank were flying to New Jersey to help the local cops there arrest Volodymyr Kovalenko and several members of his crime family. With a solid case built around him, combined with the testimony of the killer they arrested in Montana, Kovalenko would be in prison for the rest of his life.

Irritably, Dirk shifted in his seat, unable to get comfortable. Hank smirked at him. "What's going on with you? You're like a fidgety little kid."

"Nothing."

A flight attendant wheeled the beverage cart down the aisle and stopped next to Hank, further cramping their tight space. "Can I get you something to drink?"

Dirk passed the requested cup of coffee to the woman on his left. He asked for coffee as well, and Hank ordered a Coke. Dirk glared at his small paper cup, which was only half full. If the airline was afraid passengers were going to spill, they should give them lids. What was a sip and a half of caffeine going to do for him? Once the attendant pushed the cart away, they relaxed their knees, and Hank restated his question.

"It's *not* nothing. I've traveled all around the world with you, and I've never seen you so restless. What's up?"

Dirk didn't answer for a while. He'd never been comfortable talking about his feelings. Finally, he sighed. "I don't like leaving Emory and the kids. She's getting them started in therapy this week, and I feel like I should be there."

"This is a whole new you I'm going to have to get used to." Hank laughed. "Have you and the chief set a date yet?"

"Yeah. Em wants a small ceremony but with all the works, so we're looking at June."

Hank gave him a speculative side-eye. "I'm surprised you can wait that long."

"I don't want to. But there was no dissuading her mother from making a fuss. So, listen," Dirk turned in his chair, as much as he could, to face Hank. "I was wondering if you'd be willing to stand up with me, you know, be my best man?"

Hank beamed with the excitement of a child. "It would be my honor, dude!"

"Nope." Dirk shook his head. "Still can't call me dude. But thanks, man. I appreciate it."

"I'm 'man' now? Not 'kid'?" Hank teased.

"Yeah," Dirk relaxed with the levity. "Now that I've got

two boys at home who I'll probably end up calling 'kid', you've been upgraded."

"Outstanding! Do I get to pin on an insignia or anything?"

"Shut up." Dirk's lips finally eased into a smile. "I'm going to ask the boys to stand with me, too. And Emory is asking Teresa to be her maid of honor and Kendall to be a bridesmaid. Tomas and Caleb will be ring bearers."

"That's really awesome, Dirk. I'm genuinely happy for you." Hank grew solemn and sat quietly for several long minutes before he spoke. "Did I tell you I officially filed for a divorce from Amy?"

"I knew that was your plan." Dirk felt bad for his partner. Hank had been so excited to have a family, and now before they ever became one, they were splitting apart. "So, you've sent her the papers, then?"

Hank closed his eyes and rested his head back on the seat. "Yeah. We're officially over. Next, will come the custody battle. But I can't think about that right now."

"I'm sorry Hank. I know you really tried. If there's anything I can do, just ask."

"Thanks. Focusing on hunting more fugitives is the best medicine." Hank's laugh rang hollow. "Honestly, letting me be a part of your new family helps. I could never get through this without you guys in my corner."

"It's not even a question, brother."

Dirk's phone buzzed with a text from Emory. She sent a mug shot of a large dark-haired man named Seth Temple. Hank peered over his shoulder. "Who's that?"

Scrolling down the text message, Dirk said, "According to Emory, the fingerprints came back from the knife the cops found in the street after Kendall's attempted abduction, and they belong to this guy. He also has a tattoo that matches Kendall's description. He's a registered sex-offender that lives in the neighborhood next to where the Millers' house was. The reason the dirtbag sounded funny to Joey wasn't because of a Ukrainian accent as we supposed but because the guy has a lisp."

"No kidding? Well, at least they have him in custody."

"She also says that the cop who was shot during our raid is out of critical condition and is expected to have a full recovery."

Dirk clicked off the text, but his phone rang. It was Emory. "Hey, I got your text."

"Good. But there's something else." Her serious tone raised the hair on Dirk's neck.

"What?"

Kendall just got a text from an anonymous caller. It said, "Volodymyr may be out of the picture, *Myla*. But this far from over."

Icy dread coursed through Dirk's veins, and he swallowed hard. He glanced at Hank before he responded to Emory. "As soon as we land, I'll catch the next flight back home. Keep the kids in the house. I'll be there as soon as I can."

~ THE END ~

THANK YOU FOR READING **WITSEC**. I hope you enjoyed thrilling adventures with Dirk Sterling!

IF YOU LOVED READING **WITSEC**, Book 4 in the US Marshal Thriller Series, I would be most honored if you would please take a moment to write a quick review.

Review WITSEC

Thank you so much!

***

The Adventure Continues!
Next!
Book 5 in the US Marshal Thriller Series

PURSUIT

When former Army Ranger, Ian McCallum, turned contract killer, escapes FBI custody and disappears into the remote wilderness of Montana, Deputy U.S. Marshal Dirk Sterling is sent to track him down. But this isn't an everyday fugitive hunt—McCallum is racing toward the Canadian border to meet a contact who can make him disappear forever. If he gets out of the country, he'll vanish along with classified military secrets that could put countless lives at risk. Dirk must stop him—but he's not the only one hunting. Rival agencies, ruthless bounty hunters, and a private black-ops team all have their own reasons for wanting McCallum, and they don't care who gets in their way.

Back in Billings, Dirk's fiancé, Chief Deputy U.S. Marshal Emory Grey uncovers a devastating truth: McCallum's escape wasn't pure luck. Someone inside the one of the federal agencies helped him get away. When Emory starts digging too deeply, she becomes the next target. Dirk is forced to make an impossible choice—stay on McCallum's trail or race back to protect his new family and the woman he loves.

Order Your Copy of PURSUIT Today!

For free books and to join my reader group, please visit my website: Jodi-Burnett.com

ALSO BY JODI BURNETT

For more books by Jodi Burnett

Go to Jodi-Burnett.com

Flint River Series

Run For The Hills

Hidden In The Hills

Danger In The Hills

A Flint River Christmas (Free Epilogue)

A Flint River Cookbook (Free Book)

FBI-K9 Thriller Series

Baxter K9 Hero (Free Prequel)

Avenging Adam

Body Count

Concealed Cargo

Mile High Mayhem

Tin Star K9 Series

RENEGADE

MAVERICK

CARNIVAL (Novella)

<u>MARSHAL</u>

<u>JUSTICE</u>

<u>BLOODLINE</u>

<u>TRIFECTA</u>

<u>QUALIFIED</u> (Novella)

<u>TRIALS</u>

<u>SPEC OPS</u>

-

<u>US Marshal Dirk Sterling Trilogy</u>

<u>FORGED</u> (Free Prequel)

<u>EXTRACTION</u>

<u>CORRUPTION</u>

<u>REDEMPTION</u>

<u>WITSEC</u>

ACKNOWLEDGMENTS

First, and always, I thank God for blessing me with a vivid imagination, work I love, and for the inspiration with which to do it.

I remain enormously appreciative for my editing and proofreading team. I am beyond grateful to Kae Krueger who is the first to see my words and check my stories. A huge thanks to my team of beta readers who help me see the forest for the trees. You all are integral to my writing process. Thank you, Chris, Emily, Sarah, Jenni, Brooke, Sheila, Kay, Marc, and David. Thanks also to my personal assistant, Anna, without whom, I would remain an unorganized fiasco!

I am truly thankful for my writing hero, mentor, and friend, Marc Cameron for his willingness to answer questions and for his kind encouragement.

I could not do any of this without the support and encouragement of my family. Writing can be such a solo venture. Thanks for pulling me out of my cave and loving me through the rough spots. I cherish the inside jokes, all the music and sports, and most especially the way we love each other. My cup overflows.

For this book particularly, I would like to thank my grand daughter, Reilly. She helped me (and put up with my constant texting) with the current slang and teenage-girl perspective that fill the pages of WITSEC. You're amazing, sweet girl! I love you!

Most of all, I thank my husband Chris, who helps me flesh out my plots, makes sure my men sound like men, tightens up my military technicalities and lingo, and reads all the words. He listens to my crazy ideas, brainstorms with me, accompanies on my grand adventures, helps me with the business side of writing, and loves me through it all. For some reason, I struggled with the writing of WITSEC, but Chris was steadfast with his encouragement. It's because of him this book was ultimately published! I rely on his ability to see through the clouds and offer his strength. I love you, Chris, with all my heart.

Thank you everyone!

ABOUT THE AUTHOR

Jodi Burnett is a Colorado native and a mountain girl at heart. She loves writing Mystery and Suspense Thrillers from her home in the Rocky Mountains, where she lives with her husband and their two Rottweilers. There she dotes on her horses, complains about her cows, and writes to create a home for her nefarious imaginings. Burnett is a member of Novelists, Inc. and Sisters in Crime. WITSEC is her 19th book along with 5 novellas.

* 9 7 8 1 9 5 5 0 1 6 1 6 2 *